Charlie's Secret

Copyright © 2005 Alice Twiggs Vantrease
All rights reserved.
ISBN: 1-4196-0306-X
Library of Congress Control Number : 2005921051

To order additional copies, please contact us.
BookSurge, LLC
www.booksurge.com
1-866-308-6235
orders@booksurge.com

ALICE
TWIGGS VANTREASE

CHARLIE'S
SECRET

A NOVEL

2005

Charlie's Secret

ACKNOWLEDGEMENTS

A special thanks to Christopher Scott, my mentor and editor, who patiently listened to my arguments about why certain characters and events couldn't be left out of the book and understood when I left them in. Others who patiently read and commented on the first drafts: Bonnie Cannon, Martha Pike, Keith Claussen, Carol Cowsar, Susan Loudermilk and my mother Alice Wright Twiggs—all friends who read the work with enthusiasm and gave sometimes brutal criticism resulting in a much better book. Thanks also to Rucker Sterling Hennis Ph.D., Mary Ann Weathers Ph.D., China Cay Cross and Teeta Langlands whose passion for writing is infectious.

I also deeply appreciate the encouragement at the Stitch and Bitch meetings at Twiggs of Savannah Needlework and support from friends whose encouragement was needed and whose understanding of my forgetfulness marks true friendship. I'm grateful to Lou Abarr, Shirley Courter, Sandee Crow, Kay Denham, Marilyn Gignilliat, Judith Kolodny, Candace Lanier, Angela Mahany, May Mahoney, Susie Maire, Sandee Seyfurth, Maria Burns, Tamie Peters, Kay Graves, Laura Belle Macrae, Shirley Speno, Pudge Weber, Carol Goodwin, Angie Balanos, Juli Murray, Sue Ruby, Nancy Sheets and anyone else I may have inadvertently forgotten.

And thanks to Dr. Richard King and Dr. Joseph Gussler and their staff at Georgia Eye Institute who gave me back my vision and unknowingly contributed to the completion of this project.

I especially want to acknowledge my oldest living friends—Betsy Thurmond Keller, Sally Long Hendricks, Linda Lyle Walker, Gwen Gleason Lester, Gracie Merry Harison, and all others, including my children John Mulford Marks, Jr. and Sarah Elizabeth Marks—who've listened to my tall tales for years and years and years and never complained.

And how can I place a value on the input from Keith Brown, my blues-playing friend who stressed the difference between church players and club players and reinforced my belief in "root" and its enduring influence on the American South. Thanks, Keith.

PROLOGUE
Yemassee, South Carolina—1954

When I woke up that long-ago morning I had no idea that this would be the day I was to come face-to-face with someone lying in a pool of blood and about to die. It wasn't just that I was very young and unaware of such things, although that was part of it. It was more that I'd never before associated blood and death with an actual person—especially a person who was so closely connected with my life as Zerelda. Everyone I knew was alive, and mostly walking around unless they had the vapors and stayed in bed. We had pets, my brother Hank and I, and some of them had died; it made us sad for awhile, but that was forgotten as soon as new ones came along.

We kept chickens too—everyone did in the Lowcountry where we lived—and when someone said, "Let's have fried chicken for dinner tonight," we ran happily outside to help pick out the best ones to kill, and then watched them, bloody and headless running around the yard. None of this bothered us.

Neither did the slaughter of the squealing pigs that traditionally took place in October, and had actually happened a few days earlier on a cold sharp morning. Hank and I were always sent to our rooms at slaughtering time, so we wouldn't be 'troubled' by the sights and sounds; but we managed to sneak to some vantage point and see it anyway. It didn't trouble us.

No, during our far-off youth we didn't make the connection between animals dying and people dying. Death just didn't mean anything bad to us.

Yet.

***

While I don't remember everything that happened, I do remember it was still very cold on the day Zerelda died. I remember because I had dressed my ballerina doll in the same color red shirt that I was wearing. I wanted Zerelda to see us; she had made the doll's shirt to match my store-bought one. My brother Hank wore a plaid, flannel shirt and corduroy pants, but I don't remember which color. We both had on leather bomber jackets. Mine was green with a fake fur collar; his was tan and had a leather collar.

We were in school until early afternoon and Jim had picked us up as usual. His plow horse Pet pulled the wagon. She was brown and white and had a huge belly. She was always gentle. Our school wasn't far from our house, so we loved riding home with Jim, unless it was raining. We had raincoats, but they never kept much rain out. Marie had milk and cookies waiting for us when we got home that day. After we ate them, she let us play outside. "You chillun' best be home in a little while 'cause you need to do your homework," she said. Marie never let us get away with skipping homework.

I picked up my doll, and Hank and I sat on the back steps for a few minutes. We started to go down into the cellar where the furnace would keep us warm, but decided to go over to see Zerelda instead. We wanted her to read to us out of our new school book: Zerelda loved to read. So we started out on the path through the pecan grove to the cabin at the edge of the woods.

Jim and Zerelda's unpainted shack was situated on the northwestern corner of our land, out of sight of our house. There was no reassuring smoke coming from the cabin's chimney as there usually was on cold days.

When we reached the back door, we knocked loudly. Nobody came to the door; so we called out to Zerelda. There was no answer.

Hank leaned his ear against the door and said, "She must not be home. It sure is quiet in there."

"Maybe she'll be back in a minute."

"Yep. Let's sit down and wait."

So we sat and waited. It wasn't long before Hank jerked his head around and said, "You hear that?"

"No. What'd you hear?"

"I thought I heard something inside."

Now I stuck my ear against the door. Hank did too. It was as if someone was calling to us but we couldn't hear what was being said.

"It sounds like somebody is whispering to us, Hank. Can you hear it?"

"Yes, I hear it," Hank said. "Open the door and go inside, Emily."

"No. You open the door, Hank."

"No, you do it. It might be a ghost."

"It's not a ghost, it's Zerelda, you dummy. I'm not opening the door by myself." I gave him my toughest squint-eyed look. So we both pushed the door open.

It was cold and dark inside. A damp, musky odor permeated the house. We could see our breath in front of us. There was no fire in the fireplace; no kerosene lamp was burning. There was no candle lit. The cast iron supper pot that hung in the fireplace was empty. Jim wasn't there, either.

We stopped at the sitting room door and listened again. Zerelda's bedroom door was closed. As we walked toward it, we heard her whispering, "Help me. The baby's coming. Help me. Sweet Jesus, please help me."

We opened the door and saw Zerelda curled up on her side on the old iron bed. Blood was everywhere. I'd never seen so much blood. "Y'all get Marie for me," she said weakly, "the baby's coming. Please, please get Marie. Hurry."

We ran as fast as we could. My heart was beating so hard I could hear it.

Hank made it home to the kitchen door first and screamed for Marie. She came running out just as I reached the back steps. I was out of breath and gasping for air.

Hank and I were talking on top of each other: "Zerelda's bleeding, Marie. Zerelda says to hurry. Zerelda said the baby's coming. There's blood all over everything."

Marie stepped back inside to grab her coat and came running down the back steps. "Y'all go on inside now. Do your homework."

We went inside and sat in the kitchen with the laundry girl and pretended to do our homework. Adelle Jones had worked for us almost as long as Marie, except she was just a few years older than we were. "Where's Jim?" we asked her as she put some cookies and half-sweetened lemonade in front of us. "He's gone all the way to Walterboro to have that old horse shod and look for leftover horseshoes. That old horse has had more shoes in its lifetime than I have."

We waited and waited and waited. The second hand on the clock seemed to be broken. I finally put my head down on the kitchen table and was half asleep when Marie came back. She went straight to our mother's bedroom. We heard them talking, but couldn't figure out what they were saying. Marie came out and headed back to Zerelda's house. Mother yelled to us to find the phone book for her and we did. She made several phone calls after that.

Marie stayed away until later in the afternoon. She went down into the cellar for a while before coming back into the house. Her cheeks were stained with tears and she didn't want to talk much except to help us say our prayers. After that, she didn't come back to work for days.

***

We never saw Zerelda again. She and her baby died that day and they were buried soon after. We children weren't allowed to go to the funeral. Everyone else around our place did, so our dad took us over to a neighbor's house while the mourning was going on.

"It's bad enough when an old person dies, but when a baby and his momma dies—that's a tragedy for everybody," Dad said when he returned home from the service. He said he'd never seen so many people at a funeral—white or black. "After things quiet down and people go back to their own business, Jim's life will be changed. He's going to be alone now," Dad said, "You children will have to keep him cheered up."

Zerelda's death brought a change to Hank and me as well. We had lost our friend and now had no one to read stories to us, or to visit with on the long afternoons when we had to play outside. Within a few months we had learned to read, so on afternoons when Jim was home and through with his plowing we would go over and read stories to him. He spent lots of time on the porch by himself: he was an old man waiting to die, and he seemed to be happy to have our company.

Once in a while, Jim would let us ride on the back of Pet while he plowed. We usually sat on the horse backwards so it would be easier to talk to him. Although he never learned to read or write, he was a field philosopher and shared his wisdom with us. For instance, you shouldn't mix up setting hens with game chickens, or put a hungry dog next to the chicken house. Chinaberries under the house kept the moths away in summer, and finding a horseshoe meant good luck all year long—if you found the right one. That's why Jim had so many horseshoes nailed around the doors to his house. Didn't seem to help though; Jim always had bad luck.

Lots of days he liked to talk about Zerelda. "Zerelda sure

wanted that baby. She wanted that baby awful bad. Maybe it's good she's gone too, seeing that the baby died," he'd say and his eyes would get all misty. Marie said he just had rheumy eyes, but we knew better.

Some days Jim would ride us on the back of the horse until it was almost dark and Marie had to come get us. She'd always act mad and say, "Don't you know these chillun' have homework to do and baths to take? Why don't you go on home yourself?"

"Sometimes I hates to go home until dark," Jim said once. "Seems like I always see Zerelda sitting there on the porch waiting for me." I remember Jim saying that. "Seems like I always see Zerelda sitting there on the porch waiting for me."

SAVANNAH, GEORGIA
Fifty years later.

The phone rang just as I began to nod off. I knew the call was bad news even before I answered it. I'd had a juju feeling over the weekend that something bad was going to happen. The worst possible scenario, I figured, was that it would be a call from my mother threatening a visit or complaining about the insufferable May heat—anything over seventy degrees was "hell hot" according to her. I reached for the phone and said, "Hello."

It was mother. I sat down and braced myself for the conversation to come.

"Emily? That you?" My mother has a keen grasp of the obvious.

"Yes, mother, it's me. Who did you think would be answering the phone in my bedroom? What's up?"

"It's bad news, Emily. Bad news. I don't know how to tell you."

I found this hard to believe since my mother loves telling people bad news. She can't wait to get on the phone when someone dies, has an affair, or goes bankrupt. She didn't sound too enthusiastic this time, so I guessed her news must not be too bad.

"Go ahead, Mother. Tell me." I figured she had broken one of my grandmother's dishes or something.

"It's Marie, Emily. Marie's dead. I don't know what I'm going to do without her." She began to cry.

"Marie's dead? Oh my God. How did she die?"

"Old age, I suppose. The county coroner hasn't issued a final report yet, but it seems she had a heart attack and died right on the spot. Died right there on the spot in her living room."

"What about Charlie? Has anyone let him know?"

"We've been calling around trying to find Charlie, but no one knows where he is."

"When's the funeral?"

"We don't know yet," she answered, and began crying even more loudly, hiccupping between sobs.

"Let me know and I'll be there," I said and fought back my own tears. I swallowed several times, but the lump in my throat didn't go away. It just stayed there.

Mother was silent for a few seconds, and then repeated, "I don't know what I am going to do with her gone. I just don't know. Everybody is just about gone now. I don't know where I'm going to find somebody to replace her."

"I don't know either, Mother. I'll see you in a couple of days." I couldn't hang up the phone fast enough.

My mother would now face her addiction to helplessness without her nursemaid. That didn't matter to me. I was still adjusting to the news of Marie's death. I walked into the bathroom and all I could think about was that the lead horse in the family sympathy cart was dead, and I was now going to be saddled with humoring my humorless mother.

I wanted to cry, but I couldn't. I was caught in a conflict between grief at Marie's death and rage at my mother for telling me the bad news. This wasn't the first time I had fought these feelings: my mother had placed me in this position throughout my life. If I cried, I was too emotional—behaving badly. If I didn't cry, that was behaving properly, even if there was every reason to cry. When I cried, I knew I felt relief; when I didn't cry, I felt guilt. I could hear Marie saying, *Too many taboos, Emily. Your momma puts too many taboos on you chillun'.*

Marie was right. One of the biggest taboos my mother created was that of expressing or showing love for another human being. Her maternal advice was—*Be strong, Emily. Only weak people let others know how they feel.*

Today she had surprised me. She had actually cried. She felt free to share her sorrow with me, yet I was denied the same privilege. She had lost a servant. I had lost a loved one.

***

An overwhelming sense of nausea rose up in my throat and I ran into the bathroom and threw up. I washed my face when I had emptied my stomach and the nausea had finally left.

When I placed the washcloth on the side of the sink, I looked into the mirror. A middle-aged redhead stared back. I leaned closer to inspect myself for wrinkles and found myself staring into my eyes. They weren't happy eyes. They were brown, one slightly darker than the other, and I thought while everything else had aged, my eyes seemed to look back at me just the same as they had when I was sixteen. Sixteen. Too bad I didn't appreciate youth when I had it. I walked back into the bedroom. My chest felt like a professional wrestler was sitting on it, and I still had that lump in my throat. I blew my nose, then began to cry. God, I still have on mascara. It's going to run down my face. Inside my head I could hear her: *Emily, take off your mascara. When are you going to stop wearing cheap makeup? Looks like you'd try to help your appearance by buying makeup that made you seem younger. I'm glad your roots aren't showing. I don't know why you insist on dyeing your hair red.*

My mother was living rent free in my brain; I didn't need to be with her to feel the sting of her criticism.

Living in Savannah was my way of being close enough to my family in the South Carolina Lowcountry, yet still far enough away. Savannah had been my home for years, and I loved the city and the hodgepodge of people who thrived in the eclectic atmosphere of the Historic District.

My house on Abercorn Street was situated directly across the street from the Colonial Cemetery—the oldest one in the city—and gave me a wonderful view of moss-draped trees, birds, tourists and tombstones. Although the street was always busy, any traffic noises from the street blended into the chatter of tourists and tour bus drivers discussing such things as the finer points of a gentlemanly killing in the old dueling grounds at the rear of the cemetery. Smart folks, those old Savannahians, I thought. After a duel was over, they didn't have far to carry the loser; they could just haul him over to the graveyard, pop open a crypt and dump him in.

With a fire station one block away, and the police station situated diagonally across from the cemetery, I felt very safe in spite of the hordes of homeless people who slept in the small park on the corner and reveled in their drunken brawls after midnight. I didn't take any long walks after dark, though. I was glad when the days grew longer and I didn't have to leave for work when it was still dark in the morning.

School was about to let out, and for the first time in years I would have the entire summer free. This year I wasn't going to teach summer school, and I wasn't going to tutor any rotten teenaged kids who didn't want to be in school anyway. Marie's death meant I would miss the last day or so of the school year, but I didn't care. I was exhausted. I had finished grading exam papers, and I only needed to clean out the classroom and turn in my final report to complete my duties for the year.

I sat down, leaned back into my favorite chair by the window, and felt my grief wash over me again. My teaching career was uncertain; and now Marie was dead. The last happy connection to my childhood was gone. She was the one person in my life who held the key to any memories: wonderful ones, and others that were too painful to dwell on.

Thoughts were running through my head with bullet-like precision: Marie. Marie. I didn't get to say goodbye. I didn't get to tell you how much I loved you. I wanted to thank you for loving me. Marie. I loved you. Marie, can you hear me? Are you floating up there somewhere?

She had been more of a mother to me than my own—who now, in her late seventies, was still described as a beautiful woman by everyone who knew her. Her girl's body was unstooped by age. Her hair was snow white, always perfectly styled. It had turned gray when she was in her twenties and no one alive could remember what color it was when she was young. She said that as a child she had beautiful blonde, curly hair. *Not like yours, Emily. No one in my family has your coloring. You must get it from your father's side.* Her eyes were a cold, dull, violet-blue that never warmed even when she smiled.

I was over fifty years old, but when she said mean things like that to me I wanted to blurt out, "I hope so. I wouldn't want to be like you."

My mother hadn't remembered my birthday for years; Marie had always remembered. That was the reality of my relationship with these two so very different women. My mother made me itch.

I sat down in a chair at the window for a minute, then reached for the phone. I wanted to talk with my brother.

"Chandler, Cohen and McKenzie," the receptionist answered, "May I help you?"

I asked to speak to Hank and she told me curtly that he was in a meeting. "I'll call back later," I said, rather than leave a message.

My brother and I were always in the same grade at school. We were Irish twins—children born less than a year apart. He had wonderful light brown curls and greenish hazel eyes. Everyone said he was a handsome boy. I had straight strawberry blonde hair that was styled as if someone had cropped it short below my ears with a hedge trimmer. No one ever said I was attractive. Most of the time I felt invisible. I would do cart wheels, make funny faces, hop on one leg, climb trees and anything else I could do to get attention. It didn't work. As a last resort, I'd make up jokes to hide the hurt I felt inside. It kept me from crying, and it made my brother laugh. My dad would laugh too...sometimes. Mother never laughed. She'd just roll her eyes back in her head and ask someone to relieve her of my company. If I came back to the room too often, she'd haul me upstairs, order me to pull my pants down and spank me with her hair brush. It really hurt, but I refused to cry until she left the room.

After these spankings, I would spend a long time thinking of ways to deal with her: I drowned her in the creek; I pushed her down the stairs; I cut her hair off while she was sleeping; I hid her eye blinders so she couldn't take naps; I had Adelle mix up potions to make her itch. Finally, when I felt I'd exorcised her from the face of the earth, I'd feel guilty, dry my own tears and vow never to bother my mother again. Then I'd answer Marie's call to supper.

Supper was always served at six o'clock sharp. We ate in the kitchen and were usually joined there by our father. He

didn't eat with us. He liked to enjoy a few cocktails before eating. "Food puts the fire out," he said. We didn't know what he meant, but just before our bedtime our mother would join him in the den for more cocktails. By then we were already upstairs getting ready for bed.

When we finished our baths, Marie marched us downstairs to say goodnight to our parents. Then we marched upstairs again, said our prayers and went to sleep.

"Pray for someone special tonight," Marie would say.

Depending on how my day had gone, I'd pray for different things. If things were good, I'd bless each and every one. If things were bad, I'd squeeze my eyes shut and wish my enemies would step on an oyster and cut themselves, or have all their toys stolen.

Going to sleep was hardest in the summer, because the days were so long and it was still hot in our rooms, even though the attic fan was churning at full speed. A tin roof had been placed over the original shingles, so sometimes we felt as if we were sleeping in an oven. On these nights, Marie let us sneak out and sleep on the upstairs porch.

It was easier to go to sleep in the winter, when darkness came late in the afternoon and we slept snugly under warm quilts. The furnace in the cellar clanged away all night, keeping the steam heaters going. We slept long and hard back then. That was before we were afraid of dying and before Marie moved out to her own place a couple of miles down the road. The nights seemed colder and longer after she left.

***

I tried to reach Hank again. This time his secretary rang me through to him. "Hank, you've heard the news about Marie, haven't you?"

"Yes. I'm leaving in a few minutes to drive over to Yemassee to make arrangements for her at the funeral home. They called a few minutes ago. The coroner just released the body."

"Do you know how to get in touch with Charlie? He needs to be at the funeral."

"Emily, I have no idea. I'm going to ask around about him when I get to Yemassee. I'm sure Marie had his address written down somewhere. She would have been ninety-three next month, so Charlie could even be dead. He's got to be in his mid-sixties."

"Maybe so, Hank, but do try to find him. If he's still living I know he'd want to be at his momma's funeral."

Hank must have leaned away from the phone because I heard him talking to someone—probably his secretary. I didn't say anything until I knew he was back on the phone with me.

"When are you coming to Yemassee, Emily?"

"I don't know. I'll probably drive up a day or so ahead of the funeral. Let me know when you set the time. I'll be at home."

"Good. Mother says Adelle is just torn up with grief. She's going to need some emotional support too."

"Okay, Hank, but you find out where Charlie is, okay?"

"Right. Well, I've got to get a move on. My appointment at the funeral home is less than an hour away."

We said our goodbyes and I hung up the phone. I smiled and thought about how much stability he brought to my life and how much I loved him. I knew I could depend on him no matter what. He was always calm and reassuring in a crisis.

Just as suddenly as I had smiled, tears came into my eyes as I thought about Marie and the funeral ahead. "God, I hope we can find Charlie," I said to myself. I leaned back in the chair and stared out of the window—seeing nothing.

***

I was in the chair floating somewhere for a long time. I don't know how long I sat there, but it was dark when I got up. I was tired and only half awake. I yawned and walked across the room to the bathroom for a drink of water before heading to bed.

The bulb blew out when I switched on the light. I preferred to have the lights on when I used the bathroom and I wanted to wash my tear-stained face. *Put on face cream, Emily. You have too many wrinkles for a woman your age.*

There was a spare bulb under the sink. I retrieved it and reached up to replace the dead one, but I wasn't tall enough.

I didn't have a step ladder handy. Using the side of the tub, I climbed carefully up on the sink counter, unscrewed the old bulb and replaced it with the new one.

I turned around and held on to the towel bar for balance. It gave way and tore loose from the wall when I was about halfway down. I landed on my right knee. It hurt like hell. Ten minutes later it was half the size of a basketball and I could hardly move it. I had no choice; I had to call 911.

Three minutes later, the sound of sirens drowned out the heavy bass noises from rap music in the cars trolling along Abercorn Street. It was the fire truck from Station No. 31 on the corner of the next block. Neighbors were now gathering in the street, wondering where the fire was.

I was glad I was in my good robe as I dragged myself down the steps on my bottom to let the firemen into the house. My knee was throbbing, and the pain was beginning to make me nauseated. As I reached the door, I felt like a clumsy

Scarlett O'Hara leaning up to open it while swooning on the floor. So help me, God, I'll never trust a towel bar again.

Two great-looking firemen, both wearing fire pants, large jackets and helmets, came in. "Let's take a look at that leg," one said.

All I could think to say at the moment was, Why didn't I get a tan before this happened?

"Looks like you may have busted your knee cap. You're going to need to go to the emergency room. Do you want us to call an ambulance?"

I wanted so say, "No, how about some mouth-to-mouth resuscitation?" but said instead, "Yes, please, I don't want to bother my friends this late at night."

"Don't be silly," someone interrupted. "We'll take her to the hospital." That was a welcome offer from my neighbor. I didn't need the expense of an ambulance.

My next-door neighbors have been married for thirty years and are planning to renew their vows this year at the Unitarian Church. There was only one difference: while Herbert was still the same old Herbert, his wife Ginny was now Gerald. Ginny decided life as a woman wasn't fulfilling, and she'd had a sex change operation a few years ago. Herbert took it in stride and believed in honoring the marital commitment regardless of the circumstances. I sometimes wondered if that made Herbert a homosexual.

The emergency room was full. A nurse with short, thinning white hair ordered me into a wheelchair and pushed it against the wall. She handed me a pencil and clipboard with several pages of forms to fill in.

"We'll be back to take you to x-ray when your turn comes up," she said gruffly and disappeared behind a door that said 'nurses only.' I waited in the corridor. It was teeming with friends and relatives of other patients who were genuinely in need of attention, as well as home boys and several ne'er-do-wells who had no business being there.

I leaned back in the chair and shut my eyes, trying to obliterate the pain. A large black woman sitting next to me said, "What you doin' here?"

Before I could answer she said, "How'd you bung up your leg?"

"Fell."

"Me, too. Fell in the praise house. Yes'm, I fell in church during a shouting session. Couldn't help myself."

"What were you shouting about?"

"The Lord. The whole congregation was shouting. Didn't nobody know I was down until the preacher asked 'em to sit down and the music stopped. They heard me moanin' from behind the keyboards."

This was much more interesting than my fall in the bathroom, so I asked, "Why'd it take you so long to come to the emergency room?"

"The pain went away soon after the fall. I was high on the Lord and started playing again. Now it's come back. It's come back strong."

"Where do you play the keyboards?"

"First Sherman Macedonia A.M.E. Church."

"Have you ever heard of a keyboard player named Charlie Dixon?"

She pulled her brows together and thought really hard about it. "No. Can't seem to remember anybody named Charlie Dixon. He a church player or a club player?"

"I think he's a club player."

"Don't know nothing 'bout no club players. You better ask some of 'em down on River Street. Try Hugo's. They might know something about a Charlie Dixon. He straight?"

"Well, I guess so. I don't know."

"Well, if you don't know, you might try Club One-and-a-Half. Some of those he-she's down there know everything about everybody."

Before we could continue our conversation, the nurse came back for me. She looked at the chart to make sure I had filled it out, then slung it on the check-in counter. She rolled me toward the 'patient' door and unlocked it with a key secured by a conspicuous chain latched to a belt around her massive waist. She held the door open with one foot while she wheeled me through it, then rolled me down the hall and placed me in a small cubicle. She helped me on to the examining table, closed the curtain to the cubicle and left.

A young doctor came in a few seconds later. He must have been on duty for quite a while because he needed a shave; there was a bleary look in his eye too. "How did you hurt your knee?" he said.

"I fell in the bathroom changing a light bulb."

"Changing a light bulb? Were you on a ladder?"

"Nope. I was climbing off of the sink counter and the towel bar gave way. How long is this going to take, doc? I hurt, and I need to know how badly I've screwed up my knee."

He gave me the slow, bored look that tired physicians give all inquisitive patients, said, "I'll let you know after we've had it x-rayed," and left the room.

The x-ray room was the coldest room I have ever been in. I didn't have a blanket, and my teeth were chattering. "Excuse me," I said to the technician, "Can I have a blanket or something? It's cold."

The technician glared at me from behind the radiation shield, then reluctantly gave me a thin, worn-out sheet that was hanging on a tarnished brass hook on the back of the door. It was a pathetic substitute for the blanket I wanted, but I didn't complain any more. I just wanted the ordeal to be over with.

When the x-rays were completed, I was once again rolled into the hall where the black woman who played keyboards was sitting in a wheelchair.

"They find anything?"

"Don't know. Have you had your x-rays taken, yet?"

"No. Think I'm after you." She rubbed her forehead and said, "How'd you bung your knee up?"

"I was changing a light bulb in the bathroom and fell. You'd think a school teacher would know better than to climb up on a sink, wouldn't you?"

"You a school teacher?"

"Yes. I've been a high school teacher for twenty years."

"Me, too. Been substitute teaching for thirty years, but I'm getting' ready to quit."

"You are? Why?"

"Sick of it. Things have changed too much."

"What grade do you teach?"

"Seniors. West Side High school. That's why I'm quittin'. I can't straighten out uppity students anymore without gettin'

17

in trouble. Now we're dressin' them up to graduate when they can't pass the test to get out of school anyway."

"I know, but they do go to summer school and finish their work, don't they?"

She looked at me like I was crazy. "You know better than that. Most of them don't ever go back and finish. Same is true at your school. Right?"

"Right. I don't know if I'm going back to teaching next year, either."

"Humph. I'm just worn out. Plumb worn out. That's why I'm quittin'. I don't want any more parents cussin' me."

I knew what she meant. My teaching career was tenuous at best anyway, since I had made a stink about allowing failing high school students to wear a gown and walk upon the stage at graduation, even though they needed to go to summer school to complete their studies and qualify for a diploma. I didn't think failure needed any reward, but I was outvoted by others who believed that not allowing these failing students to act as if they graduated would harm their self-image forever. I was in the minority—the minority of people who understood that illiterate students with high self-esteem would have a rude awakening when they entered the job market. We had come a long way in the South, but when it came to graduating superior students, we were faking it lots of times. We had lowered our standards so far that we were now pretending to graduate non-superior students who would never complete their studies, even though they promised to do so. After leaving the podium, they would head into the streets and into the cycle of life that awaited anyone with no job skills, no manners and no future.

I kept those thoughts to myself.

"Where'd you say your friend played the keyboards?" My new friend interrupted my gloomy reflections.

"I don't know. His name is Charlie Dixon. His mother's just passed away and we need to find him."

"His mother's passed? I'll put a notice up in church. Maybe somebody's heard of him. How can I find you?"

"My name's Emily Chandler. I live on Abercorn Street and…"

A nurse appeared and wheeled my fellow teacher into the x-ray room. She came back and trundled me to my original room. I was in the cubicle for fifteen minutes before the tired physician returned. "You haven't broken any bones, but you've pulled the ligaments around the kneecap and you have some damage to the cartilage. The swelling is from the bruising. We're going to put an immobilizer cast on your leg, and you need to stay off it for the next few weeks."

"Can you give me something for the pain?"

"I'll give you a prescription," he said as he began to write on my chart. "Are you allergic to anything?"

"Nope."

"Okay," he said as he continued to write, "I'll give you something for pain. We're going to keep you in the hospital overnight to get that swelling down. I'll see you in the morning."

He called for the nurse and left the room. They talked in low voices outside my cubicle for a few minutes and then I was left alone again.

The pain was becoming unbearable. I was just about to yell out for help when the nurse returned with two strange-looking casts. "Immobilizers," she said. "We'll see which one is best."

The first cast fit. A few minutes later, another nurse came in with a wheelchair and took me to a semi-private room on the orthopedic floor. The other bed was empty. She left after helping me into the bed and making sure I had enough ice on my knee. A couple of pills later, I was asleep.

***

I didn't wake up until the doctor came in very early the next morning; it was still dark outside the window. He looked tired and his clothes were wrinkled, so I figured he had been up all night, or else he'd caught some sleep somewhere before resuming his early morning duties. He checked my knee again, made sure the immobilizer cast still fit, gave me a pair of crutches and a prescription for pain, and said I could go home.

An orderly wheeled me downstairs. I arranged to pay the bill and waited for my neighbors to pick me up.

I was groggy from the pain medication and slept most of the short way home. They helped me up the steps into the living room and eased me down on the sofa.

"Thanks for the ride, guys. I owe you one. You know y'all are my favorite couple."

They laughed like they always did, and promised to check up on me frequently. After they left, I checked the answering machine for messages. There was one from Hank saying that Marie's funeral was going to be held on Friday—two days away. I took a pain pill, lay down on the sofa and went to sleep.

When I woke up I took another pain pill and packed a few things I'd want for the trip to my childhood home and Marie's funeral. After lunch I left a message on my mother's answering machine to say I'd need someone to pick me up the next evening. There was no way I could drive myself there. Like it or not, I was going to be a hostage at Rose Plantation in Yemassee, South Carolina.

The doorbell rang. Sort of. I wasn't sure. My doorbell had a quirky personality of its own; it was like a cat and only chimed when it wanted to. No amount of tinkering seemed to help.

The doorbell rang again, more seriously this time. I reached for the crutches and pulled myself to my feet. I knew it would be Max. He was to pick me up at dusk, and if there was anything you could bet good money on, it was that Max was never late. If you said you wanted to be picked up at 6:17 p.m., Max would ring the doorbell at 6:17 p.m. In all the years I had known him, Max had never been late for anything.

Marie had stayed on with Mother out of devotion to our family (as well as a tidy monthly sum from my father's estate), but I suspected Max was there only because of the money. He had an ongoing salary from the estate and was also to receive a large sum of money from it on his 65th birthday, provided he continued to be employed by my mother. Consequently, he was happy to fetch and tote. "Yes ma'am Mrs. Chandler. Right away, Mrs. Chandler. I'll take care of it, Mrs. Chandler."

Max's other job was to make sure our place was kept up. It wasn't a hard job any more, since most of the land had been deeded to the government for tax reasons. It was now part of the National Wildlife Reserve.

Max had been hired in the sixties when he was still a hippie. He arrived one day at our house on a motorcycle, long blonde hair blowing in the wind, sunglasses, white t-shirt, jeans, big buckled cowboy belt and bare feet. He wasn't looking for a real job; he just needed a day's work so he could buy enough gas to head for Woodstock. He had a stringy-haired girlfriend with him, but I don't remember her name. She had a tattoo on her arm and just sat on the back of the motorcycle, holding on to him, looking stoned. Daddy gave him twenty-five dollars and told him to stop by on his way back and do the work he'd paid him for. My mother went nuts. "Are you crazy? You'll never see that hippie or that money again."

But we did. Max came back at the end of August to repay the debt. He never left.

His girlfriend wasn't with him. We found out later that she'd run off with one of the band members at Woodstock after getting stoned and throwing up on the stage. "I'm glad she's gone," was all he said about it.

Dad may have died young, but he was smart. He saw the true value of Max. He knew we would need lots of emotional support growing up, and it wouldn't come from our mother: she always seemed to live just one step ahead of a fit.

The doorbell rang again and there was a loud knock just as I opened the door.

Max came into the hall and looked around. "You've done some fixing up since I've been here, Emily. Your house looks good. I like the harlequin pattern you've painted on the risers to your steps. Where'd you get that idea?"

One of Max's eyebrows was raised, so I knew he was digging at me. He hated the harlequin risers.

"I was inspired by a clown I met at the circus. He had a wonderful outfit with green and white diamonds all over it. Our eyes locked and I slipped him my card. We had dinner together and the rest is history. Spent a few days in the bedroom with him and just can't get his suit out of my mind. I'm thinking about having a tent put over my bed too."

Max grinned. "You have any more luggage, Emily?"

"Nope. Just have this one bag. Besides, if I don't take too many clothes, I can come back to Savannah sooner."

"You haven't been to see us in a long while. Why do you hate to visit Yemassee? It's only an hour or so away."

"It's not Yemassee, Max. I'm just not comfortable there anymore. I don't want to stay one minute longer than I have to. If Marie wasn't dead, I wouldn't be going now. I wouldn't ever go there for any other reason than death."

"You know your mother's getting old. With Marie gone, she's going to need some help from you."

"She'll have to find it somewhere else. Being around my mother makes me too depressed. She doesn't want any help from me. I hadn't heard from her in three months until the call about Marie."

"Why do you hate your mother, Emily?" Max never minced words. He said what he was thinking.

"I don't hate her. She hates me. She always has. Now quit standing there and let's get this drive over with."

Max shrugged, took the bag from me and helped me down the steps toward the car he had been driving for years. The fading red station wagon with wooden side panels had been my mother's car first. She gave it to Max when someone asked her what it felt like to drive a 'matron mobile'. She never drove it again. Max was grateful for the gift and kept the old car in good running condition. I was grateful it wasn't going to be my mother driving.

"You riding up front or in back?" He hesitated a second then opened the back door. "You might be more comfortable in the back with that cast on your leg. Better keep it all clean and pretty like—when you get to Yemassee you can get people to autograph it."

"I'm not going to let anybody autograph my cast, Max. Are you nuts? You must have been smoking weed on the way over here."

I knew Max still liked to smoke marijuana in the evening. Mellows me out, he would claim. He was never selfish with his stash, and always offered a toke to Hank and me. I didn't participate anymore because marijuana made me sad—opened up too many doors in my memory bank, doors that I'd just as soon remain closed. Hank was different: the weed made him ridiculously happy and childlike again. He only smoked it on the weekends. If I smoked during the week, he'd say, I'd eat up all my profits. Marijuana gave Hank a terrible case of the munchies every time he used it. When he was stoned, he had the munchies worse than anyone I'd ever known.

I crawled into the back seat. Rose Plantation was at least an hour and twenty minutes from Savannah, and I needed to prop my leg up. I stretched out on the back seat, put a pillow behind my back, and leaned against the door.

Max didn't like to run the air-conditioning, said it used too much gas, so I sat forward, rolled the windows down and took a deep breath of the spring evening air. As we crossed over the suspension bridge, I leaned up further to see the lights of the city. A huge ship, flying a Panama flag, was coming up the channel of the Savannah River blowing its horn to alert the port. The skies were clear and the stars began to shine as we left the glow of the city.

"Who else is at home, Max?" I said to the back of his head.

"Just your brother. He's been by every day since Marie died. He drives over from Charleston and stays over sometimes. I suspect he'll be staying over tonight."

"What about Adelle? Have you seen her?" Adelle still worked for my mother; she washed and ironed and made sure my mother's bed linens were changed at least three times a week.

"Adelle's been by, of course. She's been in every day to check on your mother and straighten up around the house."

"Poor Adelle. I bet she's getting an earful of misery. I know how Mother hates to be in the house by herself."

"Why don't you take a nap," Max suggested, glaring at me in the mirror, "it could improve your humor."

"No thanks, Max, if I go to sleep I might miss something."

"You can't see much at night. Try to get some rest. You're not going to get any when you get home."

"I may not be able to see anything clearly, Max, but my memory bank is pretty full. I sure can imagine how the landscape looks." I sat up straighter and adjusted the pillow so I would have a clearer view of the marshes as we headed through the Savannah National Wildlife Refuge. I caught a glimpse of a blue heron. Unusual for the time of evening. Must be an alligator on the prowl.

There was a Louisiana moon—a huge yellow orb tinged with orange—lifting just above the horizon of live oaks as we drove along. It was a quiet night; few people were on the road.

I was too tired to talk. I thought about how many times I had driven this same road to and from Savannah, always dreading it. It was dark, but I knew the blue Batchelor's Buttons and purple ditch lilies were stretching their necks upward preparing to bloom, and that the pine pollen was already gone. A few late-blooming azaleas would appear here and there and the wild magnolias would be showing blooms and buds by the dozens. They were symbols of the Deep South, those magnolias.

Max seemed to read my thoughts and said, "Sure are beautiful when they bloom."

"Yes, but they're trash trees the rest of the year," I said sourly. If there's a gardening hell, it's a place where sinners are made to live under a magnolia tree that never blooms and dead leaves fall off every day of the year—forever."

"Come on, Emily, give it a rest. Magnolias are beautiful."

"Humph. Magnolia leaves are the cockroaches of the plant kingdom. If we ever have nuclear war, the roaches may survive, and I'll bet the world will still be full of tough old magnolia leaves too."

There was no more conversation after that. Max quit talking to me. He knew I was in no mood to be conciliatory about anything. I leaned back onto the pillow and shut my eyes.

***

Just before we reached home, Max said, "Emily, something isn't right about Marie's death."

Now I was awake. "What do you mean, Max?"

"When they found her dead, her house was all torn up. Drawers open. Stuff strewn everywhere. Looked as if someone was searching for something. Her bed wasn't even made up."

Now I knew something was wrong too. Marie was capable of doing a lot of strange things, but she would never die with her bed unmade.

"Was her house broken into, Max?"

"Nobody knows. The front door was unlocked, so whoever ransacked the place didn't break in. The police said Marie must have known the person and let them in—or they came in after she was dead."

"Do you have any idea what someone could have been looking for in Marie's house?"

"No. Far as I know, Marie never had much of anything

except pictures of you kids and her dolls and letters from Charlie. They said she was clutching one of those dolls when they found her. After the people at the funeral home came and picked up the body we straightened the place up, but we didn't take anything out. I didn't see a thing anyone might have wanted to steal."

"Do the police think she was murdered?"

"I don't think so. The coroner said it was pretty clear she had a heart attack." He looked at me in the mirror; I could only see the whites of his eyes in the darkness. "Murdered?" he said. "Why would anyone want to murder Marie, for heaven's sake?"

I looked back at him in the mirror and shrugged my shoulders. "I can't imagine why anyone would want to hurt Marie either. What about Doodles?" I said.

"They found him hiding under Marie's bed. He was shivering. We had to drag him out from under it."

As we approached the driveway, Max said, "Don't say anything to your mother about what I told you, please. She don't need to get all hysterical—any more than she is now. She's mad as all get out that nobody can find Charlie. As long as she's focused on that, she stays pretty straight."

Staying pretty straight meant she wasn't jumping into the liquor. She loved to drink. She never ate a meal after four o'clock in the afternoon, said it would make her fat. She could drink half the night, though. That just made her thin and mean.

***

The driveway to Rose Plantation wasn't a long one in plantation terms. The avenue of live oaks that used to line the road was mostly gone now. Summer storms and time had taken their toll. In the moonlight, the house looked the same as it always had. Tall...imposing...almost in need of a paint job, now. The lawn of winter rye was still a lush green, but beginning to die back from the heat. The ancient boxwoods edging the walkway to the front porch were clipped perfectly even. On the northeast side of the house there was a camellia garden my daddy had loved. One garden wall had fallen down and fig vine covered the space. Statues of cherubs still stood on the garden's corner posts—guarding the spot—waiting on another gardener to tend the plants and nourish the dark earth beneath them.

Two very old magnolia trees shaded either side of the house. Nothing else grew there; the trees had killed everything under their blanket of fallen leaves. It was May, though, and the magnolia buds and blossoms glowed in the light of the moon and emitted a faint, sweet fragrance. Whoever planted the trees made sure that when they were in bloom, the blossoms' delicate scent would waft through the upper floors of the house. The trees also served as a screen to prying eyes during the rest of the year—at least that's what everyone said when I'd suggested hacking them down with a chain saw.

***

My brother Hank met me at the door. "How are you, Sis?" He gave me a big hug and my eyes welled up with tears. We didn't get to see each other often—he stayed busy in his Charleston law practice—although we talked on the phone and exchanged messages over the internet at least once a week. I pulled a handful of Kleenex because my nose was beginning to run. Hank cleared his throat, "I must be catching a cold," he said huskily.

Hank was a good-looking man. He still had his curly

hair, but it was gray now. Hank was lucky in his law practice; nobody had killed him yet, he used to say. His love life was something else entirely though, with more lows than highs. He'd been married once but no children came out of it. Since then he had lived a life of sequential monogamy. Almost the same love history as me, except my marriage lasted a few years longer. Both our marriages ended in divorce. We now shared a commitment phobia.

"Mother's already gone to her room. You hungry?" Hank said.

"Sure. I could use a bite to eat. You cookin'?"

Hank gave me the okay sign with his hand and ushered me into the kitchen. Cans of tomato soup were on the counter and he had pulled the toaster from under the cabinet.

"How do cheese sandwiches and a bowl of soup sound to you?"

"Great. I'll heat up the soup."

"No. You sit down and prop that leg up. I'll fix it." He put one of the cans under the electric can opener.

"Damn it," Hank said, "This blasted thing never catches the lip of the can." He opened a drawer and pulled out a manual can opener. It worked. He turned around and winked at me. "Sis, how are you doing? I mean…besides being sad about Marie. You look tired."

"I am tired, Hank. I'm worn out. I think I'm going to quit teaching."

"You are? Does that mean you're going to retire or are you going to look for something else to do?"

"Don't know. I have enough money saved to retire if I'm careful, but I won't have much left for entertainment, so I might find a part-time job somewhere.

Hank was at the fridge pulling out cheese, mayonnaise and butter. "Do you want white bread or wheat bread?"

"White. I want a real cheese sandwich like Marie used to make."

Hank stopped putting mayonnaise on the bread and looked out of a window into the dark. I knew he was thinking about Marie too.

"What about you, Hank? How's your law practice?"

He didn't answer me. He was still staring out of the window.

"Hank? Hank? Where are you?"

He turned around and came back from wherever his memory had taken him. "What'd you say, Em?"

"I asked about your law practice. How are things going?"

"Fine. We're adding another partner soon—a female attorney who's really top notch."

"Let me guess...blonde...leggy..."

"Cut it out, Emily. No...this one's not a blonde. She's an overweight brunette, and she's not scared of anybody or anything."

"Good thing, wouldn't want you to..."

"Keep a honey where I make my money?" Hank finished my sentence.

"Right. Something like that." I knew my 'blonde' comment had irritated him, so I changed the subject.

"Have you seen Mother today?"

"Yep. She was having supper when I got here. Adelle was hovering over her, making sure she had everything she needed." Hank poured the soup and several cans of milk into a huge pot and placed it on the stove.

"Jesus, Hank. Are you planning on feeding pharaoh's army?"

"Nope. I think it'll heat up quicker in a big pot." He pulled out a spoon and began stirring the soup. "I can't remember a time when I didn't know Marie, can you?"

"Well, duhhhhhh—'course not. She was here before we were born."

"I know. I'm sure going to miss her."

"Me, too." I felt a twinge of guilt. Hank had continued to see Marie often after he moved away. I had only talked to her over the phone unless Adelle brought her to Savannah for a visit.

Marie always brought me fresh sugar cookies and lemonade like she'd fixed for us when we were young. Adelle on the other hand would usually arrive with potions of every kind imaginable—depending on what was happening in my life. When I first moved to my house on Abercorn Street, she brought me 'Coon Root'—Burglars ain't coming in the door if Coon Root's hung above it, she'd said. When I couldn't sleep well, she'd grind up dogwood and mix it with salt—told me to keep it by my bed for a safe, restful night's sleep. If nothing was going on—my usual condition—she'd give me a buckeye seed to keep in my pocket, or a packet of some ground-up leaves of what she called the Deer's Tongue plant—Black Cat w/Nine Lives was her favorite brand when she could find it. Both of these items were for luck. Keep 'em in your pocket. Don't forget 'em, she'd say.

I laughed out loud at the thought of Adelle and her potions. I knew that while Hank and I were having supper she was probably putting together all sorts of special things to help Marie on her way to Eternal Life and Salvation.

We finished eating, and Hank cleaned up the kitchen before we headed up to bed in our old rooms.

"Here, Sis, I'll help you up the stairs."

"No need. I'll just use one crutch and hold on to the rail. I can handle it. Thanks anyway."

"No problem, but I'm going to come up behind you in case you lose your balance."

The stairs were at the back of the entrance hall, behind the pocket doors that once separated the front of the house from the back. The pocket doors were seldom closed; they were rolled back and hidden in the walls unless needed. The steps circled up both sides of the wall and met on a mid-level landing before continuing in the center to the second floor. The paneled wainscoting was painted white, and the plaster walls were the color of Forsythia in the spring...a vivid, happy, yellow that was supposed to make visitors feel welcome. A door to the right side of the mid-level landing led to the old servants' quarters upstairs. They were no longer used, but when Marie first came to live with us they had served as her bedroom suite.

As I hobbled up the stairs, I ran my right hand along the top of the wainscoting. "Remember how we used to race each other down either side of the stairs to see who reached bottom first?"

"Yep. I always won until you changed the game to how quickly we could make our fingers spider-walk up the stairs."

We both laughed. While his were larger, my fingers were smaller and quicker. I always won the contest from then on.

When we reached the top of the stairs, we found our mother's bedroom door closed. This was no surprise; she enjoyed shutting us out. I was glad the door wasn't open. Hank probably felt the same way, but he just said "goodnight" and went into his bedroom.

Mine was at the end of the hall. When I turned on the light, I was glad to find very little changed. The familiar green and white toile wallpaper still hung on the walls, although the old Venetian blinds were gone, replaced with mini-shades. There was a new fabric valance too; it looked like a serpent crawling around the top of the window.

Max had placed my bag on the luggage rack, but I was too tired to unpack. My eyes hurt: not from crying, but from holding back tears. I brushed my teeth and gave myself an airplane bath—under the wings and tail—and pulled one of my old nightgowns from the dresser. It smelled of English lavender—the fragrance contained in the pink sachet in the drawer. I put the gown on and got into bed.

I lay there for a long time, but couldn't sleep. All I could think about was Charlie.

Charlie had been an important figure in my childhood. He was Marie's son, older than me: he was gone long before we loved Marie. According to her, Charlie was as smart as Einstein and as talented as Sammy Davis, Jr. Plus, Marie said, he still had both eyes.

Like Sammy Davis Jr., Marie only had one eye. She had lost the right one from smallpox as a child, but being one-eyed didn't stop her from catching us at most things we shouldn't have been doing. She wore black horn-rimmed glasses with thick lenses, so it was hard to tell she couldn't see out of her right eye. She kept her hair cut very short, and she had the roots processed every two weeks. She wasn't black or white, but somewhere in between. If she had lived in New Orleans, she'd have been termed a quadroon or mulatto. Her skin had a golden glow she attributed to some unknown Indian ancestor. Freckles were sprinkled across her nose and on her cheeks. She had perfect manners—she claimed her great-grandparents on her mother's side were never slaves, but had once been landowners with a large tract of land on Edisto Island. She owned a house near Garden's Corner on land deeded to her by an aunt. One of her ancestors, a freed slave, had claimed it after the Civil War.

Marie had worked for my family since before my birth. We always thought she was ancient, but she couldn't have been more than forty or so when she came to us.

She had been hired as a nanny because of her education. At a time when most blacks in the South were uneducated and still picking cotton, Marie graduated from high school and, after the death of her first husband, enrolled in nursing school where she earned a degree in practical nursing. Her ultimate goal was to work in a hospital, but she couldn't find a job at any of the hospitals near home; they were hiring black cleaning women, but no black nurses. "I didn't need to go to school just to empty bedpans," she said years later. After several frustrating months, she began looking through the 'help wanted' ads in the newspaper. She found our father's ad:

NURSE/NANNY WANTED for young children. Experience and references preferred. Apply in writing to P. O. Box 633 c/o this newspaper or phone 4168.

Marie answered the ad even though she had no experience as a nanny. She did have references, though. Her letters of commendation included notes from the entire staff at the St. Claire School of Nursing, three preachers, and the county undertaker who wrote that Marie had an extraordinary ability to keep her composure under extreme circumstances.

That clinched it for my dad. She started work that week, proudly dressed in her nursing uniform, shoes polished and a new gold cap on one of her front teeth. She was on duty every day from dawn to dark, with every Sunday and every other Saturday off. I wasn't born for three more months and Hank came along eleven months later, but Marie said she had her hands full from the beginning, helping mother deal with the vapors. My mother didn't take to pregnancy graciously.

Mother was talented in a sort of off-beat, helpless and seductive way, but parenting had never been one of her strong points. She always sounded a little shocked—perhaps ashamed, even—when she told people she had two children. While she attended meetings, judged flower shows and took naps, it was

Marie who dressed us for our first day at school and it was Marie who made sure our clothes were pressed and ready on graduation day.

Marie talked to us about kissing boys, flying June bugs and acting proper. She was to us the wisest person in the world, and she always listened when we talked to her. In retrospect, it was probably because she didn't have anything else to do, but in all the years she was with us she was never too busy to listen to our problems. We grew up believing Marie cared about us as much as she did about Charlie.

While she was working, Marie wore her blue nurse's uniform during the day. On formal occasions she wore a black uniform with a lacy white apron and white lace cap perched on her head. I don't think she cared much for the black uniforms.

I remember sneaking into her bedroom one night because I was scared of the dark. It was raining and the wind was blowing very hard, making the magnolia limbs scrape the side of the house. When I got to her room, I barely recognized her without her glasses and her glass eye, and she had a strange stocking cap on her head. But she held out her arms and comforted me. "Don't you let that wind worry you, Missy. That's just God's angels going 'round picking up wishes. There's lots of wishes in troubled times, and lots of angels' wings make up a lot of wind."

"Can I stay with you, Marie, until the angels are through picking up wishes?"

"Yes, child," she said and covered me with her blanket. It wasn't long before I was fast asleep. Even so, I woke up in my own bed the next morning, and when I went down to the kitchen, Marie was looking her usual self again.

***

Every time Marie's day off came around, I got anxious and asked her where she was going. The answer was always the same—either she was going to church, or she was going to Augusta to visit her sister Annie. She never wore her uniform on those days and I think she and my grandmother must have bought shoes at the same places: ugly black ones with thick soles—the kind of shoes nuns and old ladies and bridge trolls wear. She would get dressed up in a purple flowered dress with a lace collar, unless it was the First Sunday. On the First Sunday, she dressed in solid white all over: white was the chosen color of the First Ladies Club of the Briar Creek A.M.E. Church. She even wore white bridge troll shoes and white stockings.

Marie looked forward to her church meetings, but the central point in her life was her son Charlie. When he was a child, Marie told us, he went to school at Boy's Catholic in Savannah. Marie said Charlie was allowed to go there because he was so smart. When Clarence Thomas was named to the Supreme Court, she nearly burst with pride. "Charlie could have served on the Supreme Court, but he preferred music to law," she said. Marie didn't believe Anita Hill when she accused Thomas of sexual harassment, either. "No boy who went to Boy's Catholic would dare do something like that," she would declare solemnly, "'cause he'd still be 'fraid Sister Anne would catch him at it!"

After he left home as a young boy, Marie said, Charlie never wanted to come back to Yemassee. He would spend Christmas with one relative or another, and every summer at music camp. "Charlie is really playing the piano good," Marie would say. To hear her tell it, he was boogey-woogeying his way around the world. As an adult, Charlie always seemed to be going off to the most wonderful places: New Orleans—Memphis—Chicago—New York. We felt like he was mean to his momma by not coming home to see her; we figured he had the big head. The last we heard, he was playing keyboard in Diana Ross's band. That's where the stories about Charlie stopped. Marie received letters from him for lots of years, but they dried up when she got so crippled with arthritis she couldn't write back to him anymore.

Adelle said Charlie was born the same year Marie's husband, Amos, died. That was in 1935. Amos worked at the grist mill at McBean until he fell into a mill and was ground up. Since there wasn't much left of Amos to bury, the folks at the grist mill gave Marie a small pension. It took them a good while to get sales back to where they were before Amos died. Every time there was a complaint about a speck of black in their grits, someone would say, "There goes Amos." It was enough to make you sick. My dad told me there wasn't any such thing as Amos grits, and I almost quit worrying about it.

The small pension really helped Marie. It paid her way through nursing school and helped her escape the poverty many in her family had come to expect; the Civil Rights movement was still many years away, and Hampton County was about as rural as you could get in the Lowcountry. Farming and fishing were the primary occupations of most people there, white and black. But that was then.

We had lots of help in those days. It was a time before housework and yard work became demeaning. A time when milk was still delivered fresh from the farm to your doorstep. We ordered our milk from a local dairy because it was close by and because my parents liked the poems on the milk bottles. "When your children need a rest, Benson's dairy is the best. Full of vitamins and always good, Benson's tastes swell with every food." We thought the poems were stupid, but then we didn't understand poems.

Adelle cooked for us and did our laundry. She was barely a teenager when she began working for us. Several of the sharecroppers on our place were almost as old as Jim. Some of them had relatives who had been born to slaves on our place too: many even had the same last name as ours. Adelle, on the other hand, had the last name of Jones. Her family was originally from Rose Plantation, but had left after the Civil War to start a blacksmithing business. They had done well and bought a couple of acres they all still lived on. They had a sideline voodoo business that kept them occupied during the off season and any troubled times in between.

If Marie was out of town, Adelle took over as our babysitter. She was more fun than Marie, and she gave us no discipline. She was more of a playmate than a parent substitute. She didn't care if we did homework, took a nap or went to sleep on time.

Whenever our parents were out for the evening, she'd take us out into the back yard and, after vowing us to secrecy, would set off firecrackers. When the last one had burst into the night and the smell of gunpowder still lingered in the air, we would sit on the porch as she smoked her pipe and told stories—stories about how to get rid of haints and other night creatures. If you needed a houseguest to leave, you buried a chicken neck under the front steps. If you wanted somebody to sleep all night, you turned their shoes sole up and crossed them under the bed. After that, you had to walk backwards out of the room. Adelle had an answer to everything. She shared lots of other mother wit with us, but I don't remember much of it now.

She was younger, shorter, heavier and blacker than Marie, and when she smiled her grin really did stretch from ear to ear. She always wore a blue work dress and a sailor cap even when she was young. Regardless of what was happening around us, Adelle made us laugh. If we didn't eat all of our vegetables, she'd threaten us; "You better eat up," she'd say, "or I'm gonna slap a potion on you and bring all sort of boogey men into your dreams."

She sang another of her favorite warnings: "If you sings at the table and you whistles in the bed, the boogey man will get you before you dead." On evenings when we were allowed to stay up later than usual, we sometimes went outside and played a Boogey Man game until we were all so frightened we would run into the house screaming.

***

When Marie returned to work, we went back to our regular bedtime routine. Every time after that when we saw Adelle doing laundry, she'd wink at us and give a deep, belly chuckle as she patted her dress pocket full of firecrackers. We knew she was saving them for us to enjoy on her next babysitting job with us.

There was no black or white distinction I was aware of

back then, but I was young. There was class distinction, but those my parents considered lower class were just as apt to be white as black. I was in the first grade before I ever heard the word "nigger" uttered and discovered—through schoolyard education—that I was white, and that whites were supposed to be different from blacks. This was very confusing to me, because I didn't feel any different after I found out I was white.

I remember asking Marie about this when I came home from school. I was in the tub having my bath before supper and bedtime. "Marie, did you know you're a nigger?"

"What did you say?" she said.

"Did you know you are a nigger?"

She gave me a swift slap to my behind and said, "Who told you something like that?"

I didn't answer. Instead, I ran downstairs naked and screaming, "That nigger upstairs hit me."

My mother was nowhere to be found, but I wasn't looking for her. I was looking for my daddy. When I found him in the library, I yelled again, "That nigger upstairs hit me."

He was very quiet for a moment and said, "Are you using that word about Marie?"

"Yes. That nigger hit me."

He grabbed me, placed me over his knees and gave me half a dozen hard slaps to the behind. It really hurt. "Don't you ever use that word again, Emily Chandler. It's ugly. Marie is not a nigger. She is one of us. Don't ever use that word again. Don't use that word about anyone."

He took me off his knees and said, "Who told you about that word?"

"Luther Summerfield. He said we were different from... from them. He said anyone who hung around with colored people were nigger-lovers. He said Hank and I were nigger-lovers."

"Emily, Luther Summerfield is wrong. He is a small-town ignorant child with parents who are narrow-minded. He is a carpetbagger brat. Regardless of his family's money and influence here, Luther is the one who is different. He is thinking and acting like a small person."

My daddy didn't believe in mincing words; he always said exactly what he meant. You never had to worry about where you stood with him, and the spanking I received that day was the only one he ever gave me. I loved him so much it hurt, and his disappointment in me was the worst punishment I could receive. I didn't ever want to disappoint him again.

I was still sobbing, but my daddy must have known I didn't understand what he meant because he said, "Emily, people who call other people names have a small heart. It takes a big-hearted person to love everyone, in spite of any differences they may have. You have a big heart. You don't want to grow up hurting anybody's feelings, do you?"

"No, sir." I was trying to catch my breath, gulping between sobs now. Trying to quit crying, yet unable to.

"Good. Now use that big heart and go back upstairs and apologize to Marie."

I was less confused, but still had tears in my eyes. Perhaps a little ashamed too. I had just had my first lesson in Southern diplomacy.

Marie was still sitting on the stool next to the tub when I returned. She had her head in her hands, but looked up just as I reached the top step.

"I'm sorry, Marie. I'm sorry." I remember how easily the apology came because I knew I had hurt her.

She held out her arms and wrapped a towel around me,

then held me close. "Missy," she said, "trash is trash. It don't matter which color it is. If you always remember that, you'll be able to separate the wheat from the chaff. Trashy folks are always trying to bring other folks down to their level of trashiness. It's harder to climb up and clean up, than it is to slide down and wallow in the dirt."

The wheat and chaff bit didn't mean anything to me, but I understood the message about trash, climbing and cleaning up. I also remember the momentary sadness in Marie's eyes when she spoke to me that day. I was too young to realize her sadness was caused by my first exposure to racism in the heart of the land she called home too.

We never discussed it again, but I knew she remembered it until the day she died. Some things you just can't take back. I think mean words hang back somewhere in your memory, waiting to be called on to remind you to feel guilty or ashamed. So do sad things that happen in life—like Zerelda dying and Jim mourning her the rest of his days.

Whenever I thought about babies I remembered Zerelda lying in a pool of blood calling for help. Even though I was too young to attend the funeral and I wasn't allowed to see them, I could picture Zerelda lying in the casket with her little dead baby placed in her arms.

Lots of people were having babies when I grew up, but after that time I never thought about babies being born alive: I only thought about dead ones. Whenever a friend went into labor I was anxious until someone reassured me the mother and baby were doing fine; only then would I go to the hospital and visit.

About the same time Zerelda died, Marie's sister Annie had a baby she named Jesse. Everybody was excited, because Annie and her husband had wanted a baby for a long time. Marie was finally an aunt. She was really proud of that baby and talked about him all the time.

"Jesse didn't weigh but three pounds when he was born and Annie keeps him wrapped up in a hand towel," Marie said. Annie kept the baby warm in a shoebox in her dresser drawer until he got big enough to use a baby bed. Marie said he cried a lot when he was first born, but that helped his lungs grow stronger.

Annie carried the baby with her everywhere she went. "She never leaves that baby at home," Marie said. "He can't get any sleep 'cause she's always taking him out on a visit somewhere to show him off."

In spite of his continuous outings, Jesse thrived. "He's the happiest baby you ever saw," Marie used to say. "All he needs to be happy is a bottle full of milk."

Annie had lots of baby bottles, but Marie worried about his diet…said Annie sometimes fed him with a rubber nipple jammed onto a coke bottle full of unpasteurized milk. Later she fretted he would choke on the drumstick bone Annie let him chew when he was teething.

As he grew and developed, Jesse continued to be the happiest baby anybody ever saw, according to Marie. "That baby is so smart, he's gonna be just like my Charlie."

I remember meeting Jesse for the first time. He and his mother came to spend Easter with Marie. Marie's sister had a car, so they arrived to pick Marie up from work when they got into town.

When Hank and I heard the car coming down the driveway, we ran to the kitchen window. The windows in the kitchen came all the way to the floor—remnants of a Victorian makeover—so we didn't have to stand on tiptoes to look out.

The car was a Buick—black with lots of chrome on it. It was so shiny Marie said we needed our sunglasses to look at it. As the car came to a stop, Marie's sister stepped out and then held out her hand to help her son out of the car.

"Can you see him, Hank?"

It was a bad question to ask, because even though he was taller and could see over my shoulder, Hank pushed me out of the way and said, "Yep. I see him."

"What's he look like?"

"He looks just like me and you."

"He does?"

"Yep."

"He's not black?"

"Nope."

"What color is he?"

"Almost just like Marie."

It was true: Jesse was almost like Marie. Brown curly hair, dark eyes, and skin that looked just like Marie's, except lighter. He was dressed in dark green corduroy pants with plaid flannel lining. He was smiling so we knew he was okay.

As Marie went out the back door to greet them, we followed her. Hank walked right up to Jesse, but I stayed behind Marie's skirt until she introduced us.

"Emily. Hank. This is Jesse. He is four years old. Y'all play outside while I get my things." She and her sister then went up the steps into the kitchen.

Jesse smiled at us. I smiled back at Jesse, but Hank didn't.

"What do you like to do, Jesse?" Hank said. Hank was all business when it came to meeting people.

Jesse squinted his eyes and pressed his lips together. We could tell he was thinking.

"I like to be windshield wipers," he finally answered.

"Windshield wipers? Did you say windshield wipers?" Hank was stupefied. "How can you be windshield wipers?" he asked.

"Easy." Jesse ran back to the car and pulled the driver's side door open. He disappeared into the back seat before climbing back out with a fist full of silver-colored wiper blades.

"See. These are Cadillac wipers. They go like this." Jesse swung the blades from right to left in unison.

"This is when you don't have much rain." He moved the blades very slowly. Then he moved them faster. Then faster and faster and faster.

"This is when you have a lot of rain."

He stopped for a moment, picked up another pair of blades and pushed them back and forth in different directions— toward each other and then away from each other. Toward each other and then away from each other.

"Now these are Studebaker wipers."

Before we could comment, he began swinging the blades up and down, to and fro, backwards and forwards. His movements made us dizzy.

"What are you now?" Hank said.

"Broken," he said and fell laughing to the ground.

We laughed with him, and after Jesse was back on his feet we spent the next few minutes playing like we were windshield wiper blades too.

We were ten years old and Jesse was only four, but he was already a leader. We were sad when his mother and Marie came back out, because we knew they were getting ready to leave.

"Jesse, grab up your things and let's..." Marie didn't finish her sentence. Another black car was coming down the driveway. It was Luther Summerfield and his mother in their big Packard, followed by a huge cloud of dust churned up by their driving too fast down the avenue of oaks that led to the house.

Without saying another word, Marie and her sister pushed Jesse in the car, slammed the doors and started the engine. They were ready to go as soon as the Summerfields parked their car. As Marie's sister drove away I knew Marie was telling her about "that Summerfield white trash."

Luther and his mother stayed in their car until the dust settled, then she got out.

"Hello, Hank. Hello, Emily. Where's your mother?" Mrs. Summerfield said.

"She's taking a nap," I said.

Hank rolled his eyes at me and I crossed mine at him. Mrs. Summerfield had on a black and white polka-dotted dress, ugly black shoes, a black hat and red Betty Boop lips.

Our mother came out then, and she and Mrs. Summerfield talked about flowers. Luther stayed in the car with his nose pressed against the window. He had just started junior high school and was wearing khaki pants and a plaid shirt. Hank wanted to throw a stink bug in the car with Luther, but I didn't. I didn't like bugs and I didn't hate Luther enough to pick one up, so we stuck out our tongues at him and ran into the house, happy to have escaped the situation.

After that, Marie always went to Augusta on holidays to visit her sister and Jesse. We missed her every time she left.

We didn't see Jesse many times in the following years, but we talked on the phone to him whenever he called Marie, and we always swapped Christmas presents and remembered each others' birthdays.

***

While Jesse was growing up, Marie kept us informed about him. We knew he made straight A's on his report cards, sang in the choir, played quarterback on his high school team, and received a scholarship to college. His mother didn't like any of the girls he dated. He worked for three whole summers to save the money to buy his first car.

"Jesse's got a brand new car," Marie told us. "He bought himself a red convertible. A red Chevrolet convertible and he's going to take me riding in it."

Marie sure was happy when Jesse bought that car.

"Doesn't seem fair, does it?" Hank said to me back then. "He has a brand new car. At his age, I had to leave mine parked with the engine running or find a hill to park on if I wanted to go somewhere."

Another of Marie's happiest days was when Jesse finished college. She took a week off to participate in the event, and when she returned to work she announced he was going to medical school. "Jesse's gone and gotten himself another scholarship," she said proudly.

When he finished medical school and became a physician, Marie made sure he sent invitations to each of us, and we went to his graduation with her. He did his residency in oncology at Mt. Sinai Hospital in New York City, and returned to teach and practice at the Medical College of Georgia where he had graduated several years earlier.

Seeing Jesse again was about the only thing I was looking forward to in the coming days. Marie's funeral was going to be a difficult time for all of us.

On the morning of Marie's funeral, I went down to breakfast early. Max was already in the kitchen and feeding Doodles by hand. "Doodles won't eat, Emily, he must be grieving too."

"Who's going to be taking care of him after the funeral, Max?"

"Don't know for sure. Everybody's been taking turns so far. Doodles is a fine little dog. Smart, too. Why don't you take him? He'll sleep in the bed with you and keep you warm."

"Great suggestion, Max. I should have slept with more dogs and fewer men. I just might take him home with me."

"Yep. Doodles might be the kind of male you need in your life. No balls. Happy to see you every time you walk in the room. Grateful for any food you feed him...Yep...it's just about the perfect match...you and Doodles.

"Go to hell, Max. What do you know about relationships? You haven't had a girlfriend in years." Max grinned, leaned back in his chair, cocked his head and said, "That's what you think. Sounds like you need Adelle to mix you up a relaxin' potion."

He went on, "You sure are uptight today. You might be too uptight for Doodles. You might make him nervous. He's used to a calm woman like Marie."

Marie had found Doodles foraging for food inside a turned-over garbage can at the back of her house when he was just a puppy. He was skinny, shivering, and starving, but she scooped him up and took him to the vet right away. He didn't have any major problems and, with his shots updated and lots of tender loving care, Doodles turned into a roly-poly little dog. The vet said Doodles was half poodle and half American yard dog. He was neutered when he was six months old, and he stayed by Marie's side constantly. His only vice was to hump a stranger's leg whenever the opportunity arose.

Doodles and Marie went everywhere together. When Marie came to work, Doodles came to work. When Marie went to church, he went to church too. He even went to her funeral.

***

Marie's funeral was scheduled for 2 p.m. at Briar Creek A.M.E. Church. The little clapboard church sat on the side of a hill—it always seemed as if it was going to fall into the pluff mud along the creek. A few large live oaks surrounded the church, and the Spanish moss was especially thick since it received extra moisture from the humidity of the creek.

I had kept my emotions in check since returning home, dreading the funeral. *Emily, don't be such a sissy. Everybody has to die. Are you wearing that to the funeral? I wish you didn't have those hideous crutches to contend with. It's just like you to break your knee at a time like this.* My mother's voice was working overtime in my brain.

It was a sunny day, but several dark clouds on the horizon promised rain later. I decided to wear a beige linen dress to the funeral; it was loose and comfortable and made walking with a bum knee easier. Wrinkled linen was no problem. I didn't wear a hat. In deference to Marie, however, I wore the largest, loudest pair of earrings I owned.

I rode with Max and Doodles. I appreciated Max's patience and help getting in and out of the car. Everyone else rode with my mother. She was indignant that we were taking a dog to a funeral.

We arrived early, just ahead of the paid mourners and the Ladies' Auxiliary, of which Marie had been a member. Marie's Auxiliary members were dressed all in white, from their patent leather shoes to their hats, complete with feathers of every size and description. Max had arranged for the Evans Family Quartet to perform at the funeral, and they had begun warming up their voices. They were wonderful singers; somehow I knew this would be a toe-tapping, hand-clapping send-off for Marie.

The church, now painted white, had been established in 1865 by freed slaves. Several members could still trace their ancestry back to that time. The building was dimly lit but streams of sunlight through the windows accentuated the warm honey tones of the heart pine walls and pews. An old upright piano sat in the corner. The piano player was an ancient woman who stooped over the keys and seemed to be half asleep. The choir sat in folding chairs in the balcony overhead. Marie's Society members sat together on the left side of the aisle. Several other societies were also in attendance. The paid mourners began to warm up, clutching at handkerchiefs and dabbing at their eyes. A few were beginning to moan, and one mourner was helped to her seat because she had managed to work up enough grief to convince the pallbearers she was having a serious medical problem. They motioned to the funeral home nurse and she came over with a small bottle that must have held ammonia because I could smell it. The nurse said, "Take a deep breath," as she held it under the woman's nose. It worked, because she gasped, snorted, sat up, put her hat on straight and began to cry all over again.

Tears were beginning to well up in my eyes too, so I put on my sunglasses. Marie. Oh, how I will miss you. I wish I could let loose and express my feelings too.

I was surprised at the number of people in the church. Marie's circle of acquaintances was more varied than I had realized. Marie's sister Annie, Jesse, and Adelle all sat together in the front row. Annie was smart in a black dress, pearls, and a wide-brimmed white hat with black roses. Jesse was wearing a dark blue suit and looked just the same as he always had—tall, handsome and sure of himself. Adelle wore a flowered dress and her customary sailor cap. I couldn't see her pipe or her firecrackers, but I knew they were hidden on her somewhere. She had gone up front to view Marie, and I saw her place something in the casket. I know others saw it too, but no one said anything.

Adelle's cousin, a renowned voodoo doctor in the Lowcountry, sat at the rear of the church. Several other people I did not know were seated with him; I presumed they were part of the voodoo culture as well. Although he was now dead, the original Dr. Buzzard—the Lowcountry's most renowned voodoo practitioner—was still revered by anyone who dabbled in potions and haint management. Dr. Buzzard had come to fame almost accidentally. Local legend said when he was just beginning to practice black and white root, he put a spell on one of the fishing boats that went out to sea one long ago day. A storm blew up and all of the boats turned over and the occupants were drowned—all of the boats except one: the boat Dr. Buzzard had put a spell on came back to shore safely with a buzzard sitting on its bow. He was called Dr. Buzzard from that time forward. His fame spread, and to this day South Carolina voodoo is said to be the most powerful there is.

Adelle dabbled in voodoo part-time. She was extremely superstitious, and passed along many of her fears to my brother and me when we were children. Marie believed in voodoo too.

This part of Marie's life was one I was not privy to, but

respected. Despite her life with us, she had a strong attachment to the customs of her culture.

Her plain casket was open. Those of us who wished to do so were invited to walk down to the front and view the body. I didn't want to look at Marie. I remembered looking at my daddy in his casket: since then, it had been hard for me to remember him alive. I could conjure him up if I tried long enough. But now whenever I thought of people in a casket, I saw them lying there with their eyes shut and wondered if they were fully clothed below the waist—and if they weren't, what would happen on Judgment Day.

I don't want to see Marie in the casket. I want to remember people as they lived. Once I look at her in the casket, that's all I'll remember. I can't do it. I won't do it.

***

As the church began to fill up, Max went in with Doodles and took a seat. I stayed in the back watching the crowd. I knew I would soon have to go in and sit down too, or walk on up front and view the body. Easy decision. I'd crutch it on in and take a seat while trying to look as if I was in severe pain. As I entered, I felt every eye in the place on me as if they were wondering what my decision would be. Should I go and view the body? Should I just politely take a seat? I knew what Marie would have done. She would 'fall out.' That happened when you were so overtaken with grief you just fell out of your seat and collapsed in the aisle. You could also 'fall out' when you looked into the casket. I had vowed to be strong. I wasn't going to 'fall out.'

I sat down on the end of the row next to Max and Doodles. Hank and my mother sat in the pew in front of us. It was very quiet. The only sounds were my crutches clanking onto the floor as I put them down, and the barely audible whirr of hand-held fans—they had the imprint of the funeral home on the back and a picture of Jesus on the front. Doodles began to pant, and a few of the older men cleared their throats. I could still sense people staring at me from behind, and I figured they were waiting on me to go up to the casket.

Several people were going up to the front to view the body. One said, "Don't she look natural."

"She is asleep in Jesus," said another.

I quit listening after that. It was too painful.

***

Just before the service began, someone nudged me over. It was my childhood friend Greg Campbell. He was now the High Sheriff of Hampton County—that's what Adelle called him. Any other type deputy was a low sheriff. I took one look at him and began to cry. I couldn't hold the tears back any longer. Greg had loved Marie too, and I knew he was there to offer me moral support. He had been my high school sweetheart and I had heard he was recently divorced. I hadn't seen him in twenty years.

He took my hand and that's when I began to sob out loud, and leaned over against his shoulder. My mother turned around and gave me a dirty look, but I couldn't quit crying. I was glad I had a pocketbook full of tissues; it looked as if I was going to need every one of them.

The church was decorated with white ribbons and roses of every description and color. Some of the flowers were real; others were made of plastic. The piano player was playing chords, slowly setting the mood of the crowd for the upcoming service.

All of a sudden there was a piercing noise. The fire alarm

had gone off. Beep…beep…beep…beep. Nobody moved. Everyone kept talking as if a fire alarm was a normal thing to go off at a funeral. A couple of young girls at the front of the church began to clap their hands in unison with the alarm, sometimes adding an extra clap in between the burst of noise as if they were at cheerleading practice.

A man sitting behind us said, "What time is the funeral supposed to begin?"

"About now," someone answered.

Suddenly the piano player began a grand crescendo of chords and everyone sat up straighter in their seats. The young girls were still keeping time to the unrelenting beep of the fire alarm.

"Greg, is she trying to drown out the fire alarm, or is this the beginning of the service?" Before he could answer the fire alarm stopped, and the young girls slumped back down in their seats.

Marie had said the Bishop was an old man, but was no slouch when it came to preaching. She was right. He seemed somber as he entered the church. His very presence commanded reverence, and he carried an aura of spirituality. He was dressed in his purple robe and today he was carrying a white Bible. The congregation stood up in respect. The piano player, now fully awake, slowed down her chord playing, and the bishop began to speak.

"We are gathered here today to say goodbye to Sister Marie. Amen. Say Amen."

The congregation said, "Amen."

"Did I hear Amen? Praise the Lord."

"Amen. Amen."

The piano player had nodded off to sleep again, but someone nudged her and she struck up a rendition of "When the Saints Go Marching In" before she realized we weren't at that point in the service yet, so she quickly stopped and began playing "Precious Memories."

The service was short and sweet, with the choir singing "Touch Me Lord Jesus" and "Precious Lord." The Evans Family Quartet performed "Sit Down, Servant" and "He's Got the Whole World in His Hands." The service ended with the bishop inviting everyone to meet in the cemetery for a final farewell to Sister Marie and the piano player banged out a complete version of "When the Saints Go Marching In."

***

As we left the church I noticed dark clouds were beginning to gather overhead, even though the thunder was still a long way off. "Sometimes I Feel Like A Motherless Child," I started humming to myself, but I choked on it. Since Marie was being buried in the church graveyard, we stood respectfully while the pallbearers moved the coffin to the stand underneath the tent.

Hank said, "I hope it doesn't rain until later."

Greg leaned over and whispered, "Don't tempt the devil. If you don't notice the clouds, they won't turn loose."

Doodles saw a squirrel and ran off to chase it. Max caught up with him and put him back on the leash as we headed to the graveyard. It had been cleaned up for the ceremony—all of the old flowers had been carted away, and new arrangements, mostly plastic, were settled in their place.

Thank goodness there were enough seats under the tent for everybody. The paid mourners had worked themselves up to a high pitch and were leaning on anyone they could clutch. Jesse motioned for us to join him. Max led Mother carefully down to the front row and they took their seats. By now she was ignoring me completely. She didn't speak to Greg, either. She had hated him when we were in high school, and from her dismissive behavior nothing had changed.

When everyone was seated, the bishop cleared his throat and began the graveside service. It ended with a prayer and everyone singing "Amazing Grace."

Greg retrieved my crutches from under the chairs and we walked up front to give our respects to Jesse and his mother. As we walked to Max's car, Preston Floyd, a local lawyer, approached us. "Emily, we are going to have the reading of Marie's will tomorrow, and I need for you to be there."

"You want Emily there?" my mother chimed in. "I can't believe Marie would want anyone at the reading of her will except Jesse and Charlie, if we could find him."

Preston ignored the interruption. "Emily, can you come by my office around ten o'clock in the morning?" My mother turned around in a huff and left.

I told Preston I would be there on time, and headed to Max's car. Greg opened the door, helped me in and said, "Emily, I need to get back to work, I'll see you later." He didn't wait for my answer. I guessed he'd had as much of our family as he could take in one day. I wanted to run after him and escape everything for a few hours. Damned crutches. Why couldn't this be happening when I had two good legs?

Hank gave me a ride into town the next morning. We rode along in silence until we passed the old slave cemetery on River Road. A huge live oak tree had blown over during a recent storm, and now you couldn't see any of the grave markers.

"Hope someone moves that tree out of the way soon. It looks like the big tree that fell was the one behind Jim and Zerelda's graves," Hank said.

"Damn, Hank. I haven't visited their graves in years. I'm ashamed to admit it, but I haven't. Is anyone living in their old cabin?"

"Nope. No indoor plumbing, remember? We're going to have to tear it down or move it when the road is widened."

"You're not going to tear it down are you?"

"Nope. Move it."

"Where are you going to move it ?"

"Thinking about putting it down by the stream and using it as a hideaway. It's old, but it's solid. Still has some of Jim and Zerelda's furniture in it."

"Are you going to keep the blue shutters and door when you move it?"

"Yep. Might have to scare off some swamp haints." Hank laughed and patted me on the knee. "Or one old daffodil hag I know."

"Gee, thanks, Hank. Daffodil hag? A hag? That's a fine name to put on me at my age. I feel old enough as it is without your reminding me."

"I'm just kidding, Em. You look pretty good for a sister."

I gave Hank the best cross-eyed look I had, and knuckle

rapped him as hard as I could on his upper arm. "You better not be planning on having any of your blonde bimbos down at that hideaway, Hank, or I'll turn into a real hag and come skulking around and warn them of your true intentions."

"Speaking of skulking around, Emily, did you ever wonder why Marie spent so much time in the cabin after Zerelda died?"

"Nope. Just figured she was taking supper to Jim."

"I'm not talking about when Jim was living. She kept going down there after he died. She spent hours there. Don't you remember? Always saying she was checking on things. Making sure everything was okay."

"Gosh, Hank, that was years and years ago. Maybe she wanted to sit and visit with the memories there. That's all."

"Maybe so. But when I finally said something to her about it, she just told me to mind my own business."

"How long did she keep going there?"

"Quite a while—she must have been in and out of there for three or four years after Jim died, but eventually she stopped. Funny thing, though. She made another trip down there two weeks ago. Adelle was with her. I stopped and teased her when I drove by and saw her coming out of the cabin, but she didn't say anything to me—just gave me an irritated look. She couldn't drive any more, she couldn't go anywhere unless Adelle took her. I wanted to give her a hug, but she just glared at me and put her big pocketbook in Adelle's car and they drove off."

"Marie loved those big bags, didn't she."

"Yep. But she was carrying bigger and bigger bags in those last days."

"Wonder what she was doing there?"

Hank didn't answer, so I continued talking, "Do you

remember when Zerelda and the baby died? It was awful, wasn't it."

Hank still didn't answer. I looked over and his eyes looked all misty, so I didn't say anything else. When we reached the court house, Hank helped me out and onto my crutches.

"You need a ride home, Sis?"

"Nope. I'll catch a ride with Jesse. Thanks anyway."

***

I was early for the meeting with Preston, and I went into the courtyard to wait. The courthouse had been redone during the bi-centennial celebration, and all the charm had been reconstructed out of it. It reminded me of the center building in a strip mall. Even the clock in the clock tower had been remodeled until it looked like a plastic replica of the real thing. The fig vine coverings were gone, and the replaced mortar between the bricks almost sparkled in the sunlight. The courtyard was all spiffed up with new gardenia plants and a serpentine brick sidewalk. The wrought iron benches were the only things that still looked authentic: they had new wooden slats, but the wrought iron still had the roughened, dark patina of Old Savannah green. I wondered if the pigeons were new too.

I sat down to people-watch and regretted not having brought more clothing with me; I was going to have to stay in Yemassee longer than I had first planned. I was wearing a floral Lily Pulitzer sundress I had pulled out of the closet in my old room, and I had a red sandal on my good foot. The sandal didn't match my dress, but I didn't care. I leaned my crutches against the back of the bench and waited.

The heady scent of gardenias surrounded me, and I was about to start daydreaming when I saw Luther Summerfield standing across the street talking to someone I didn't know. I hadn't seen him since we were in high school; he was three grades ahead of Hank and me.

Luther came from a prestigious family of enthusiastic social climbers and back-stabbing politicians. He was the weirdest person I had ever known. Not weird in a sadistic sort of way, but weird in an eccentric sense. Nasty, too.

While he continued his conversation with the stranger, Luther managed to turn around so he could stare at me and talk at the same time. That jerk is trying to figure out who I am. He's still the nosiest person in town. I hope I'm lucky and he keeps his weird self across the street.

Luck wasn't with me. Luther ended his conversation, crossed the street and headed in my direction.

***

The courtyard had a circular walkway that went around a monument to commemorate those who'd served in any type war. The benches, placed evenly around the outside perimeter of the walkway, were empty except for a few old men feeding the pigeons. English ivy covered the ground beneath the large purple Indica azaleas, still sporting blooms on a few branches. A large clump of Spanish moss cascaded across the walkway near the fountain that stands by the side entrance to the courthouse.

Luther walked counter-clockwise around the courtyard circle so he could pass my bench and stare at me head on. Drop dead, you jerk, was all I could think.

Luther was just under six feet tall. He was wearing a pair of dirty navy blue shorts, a paint-streaked gray t-shirt, and work boots without socks. His once-blonde hair was graying; and he attempted to disguise his bald spot by parting his hair just above his left ear and combing it all the way over to his right ear. His watery blue eyes were hidden behind a thick pair of sunglasses that were threatening to fall off the end of his nose. It was obvious he was still trying to remember who I was.

I decided to ignore him. I could tell he was getting close because he was wearing the type of cologne you can smell from twenty feet away. It sure wasn't Old Spice: it seemed to be some sort of musk cologne mixed with diesel fuel. It stunk.

Before Luther could circle around the courtyard again, Jesse appeared. He was dressed casually but was wearing a sport coat. "You ready?"

I nodded yes, and we walked around the side of the courthouse to the row of small offices behind it. They had been adapted from the original Charleston and Western Carolina railway station. That was the line that used to carry passengers from Augusta to Beaufort before they tore up the tracks.

***

Preston Floyd's country-lawyer office was nicely furnished. The chairs in the waiting room were leather—new leather. Mahogany side tables gleamed with polish, and they were topped with brass lamps. The only give-away that Preston wasn't used to this type of luxury was the plastic covering that had been left on all of the lamp shades. "Keeps the dust off," his secretary explained. She pointed to the chairs and told us to take a seat—Preston would be right out. I couldn't take my eyes off her long red fingernails. They were so long I wondered how she could type. I also wondered how she could walk anywhere in her spiked red high-heeled shoes.

We didn't have to wait. Preston walked out into the waiting room, shook hands with Jesse, and motioned for us to come into his office. All of his law books were new too. Didn't look like any of them were used much.

"Have a seat. This won't take long, since Marie didn't have a lot to leave anybody." He placed his reading glasses on the end of his nose and took the one-page will from the folder. "I, Marie Dixon, being of sound mind and body…" She'd left everything to Jesse except for her steamer trunk, which she willed to me along with any personal things Jesse didn't want. She didn't leave anything to Charlie.

As soon as he finished reading the will, he paused, lowered his eyes for a moment, and then looked directly at me. "Marie also said for me to personally tell you Charlie has a secret and it is an important one."

"Secret? What kind of secret?"

"I don't know. She wouldn't tell me, but she was adamant I was to tell you that. She said you'd find Charlie sooner or later."

"Preston, I've never met Charlie. I don't even know how to get in touch with him. He has been gone for years. He's over sixty years old by now, and obviously he doesn't know his mother has passed on because he didn't show up at her funeral."

"I know, but Marie was quite definite about it. She said it was important for you to find Charlie."

I was silent for a moment. I was confused. Why didn't Marie leave anything to Charlie in her will? If she had his address, where would I find it? And why in the hell did he treat his mother the way he did? Just abandoning her like that?

The attorney interrupted my thoughts, "Marie didn't leave Charlie anything because she said he wouldn't know the difference when she was gone. I asked her how to get in touch with him, but she kept saying you would find him. It's a puzzle to me too."

Jesse hadn't said anything at all since the will had been read. I could see he was deeply disturbed.

"What's the matter, Jesse?" I asked, "You know how much Marie loved you. You were her sister's only child. It stands to reason she would leave you almost everything in her will."

"That's not what is bothering me, Emily. I'm thinking about Charlie. I never met him, either. I read lots of his letters when they came to her. I listened to her tell my mother how well Charlie was doing and who he was working with. I feel just the same as you, I don't know why he treated his mother like he did. Maybe he's dead too."

Jesse grew silent again. Neither Preston nor I wanted to break into his thoughts. All I could hear was the grandfather clock. Tick...tock...tick...tock...tick...tock.

After a minute or so, Jesse stood up and looked at me. "We might as well head home. If you are going to find Charlie, there's no time like the present to start looking."

Preston told us he was filing everything with the probate court within a few days. He leaned back into his chair and said, "Good luck to you. I never met Charlie, either, but I knew his daddy well. He was a fine man. Shame he was ground up in that grist mill."

We thanked him for his time and left. The dark clouds gathering in the sky promised a heavy rain, so we hurried home. We didn't talk at all on the drive back, and Jesse wouldn't stay for dinner, said he was going to be on call all weekend and had to get back to Augusta.

He walked me to the door and opened it.

"Wish you'd stay for dinner, Jesse," I said once more.

Jesse didn't answer. He smiled and then he was gone.

Hank had a drink waiting for me. "What happened at the will-reading today?"

"Marie left everything to Jesse and her old steamer trunk to me." I sat down and took a sip of my drink then leaned forward in my chair. "The strangest thing happened. Marie left a message for me with her attorney. She said it was important that I find Charlie. She didn't leave any other information at all."

"Maybe you'll find something at her house."

"Maybe so. I'm going out there tomorrow."

"Tell you what. I'll make a few calls to some friends and see if I can get a lead on Charlie too. One of the attorneys in our office may know something. We've handled a few copyright infringement cases for the record companies; there could be a connection there."

"Thanks, Hank. We need to find him right away. Marie's message said I would find him sooner or later, but I swear I don't know where to begin looking."

A few drinks later I asked about Luther. "You remember Luther Summerfield?"

"Yes, 'course I do," Hank said. "Luther is just the same as always."

"He looked weirder than ever when I saw him today in town, and he was dressed like a derelict. He was circling around the courtyard trying to figure out who I was."

Hank laughed. "You remember when his mother used to have him chauffeured to school? He wore sissy suits with knee socks, Buster Brown shoes and a beret."

"Yeah, and she had a fan installed in the back of that old Bentley so he wouldn't get too hot while he rode in the car."

"How about his museum?" Hank said, and we both doubled up with laughter. I laughed so hard the muscles on my sides felt like I'd pulled them loose.

Luther's museum had always been fodder for community laughter. He had collected junk of all shapes and sizes as a child, and continued junk-collecting as an adult. The only difference between then and now was that at some point he had added tabby remnants and concrete slabs to his piles of junk. He had inherited a ten-acre plot of land from an uncle, and kept all of his treasures on the site. A six-foot chain-link fence surrounded the property, and Luther had it electrified to keep any junk robbers at bay. He used a fork-lift to move most of the stuff around, and rented a crane whenever he needed to re-arrange anything really heavy. He kept an inventory of each item with details of exactly where it came from, the date he found it, what it was made of, and the exact section where he'd put it in his museum.

Max swore he had seen Luther stop by the side of the road one time and pick up a pile of rocks, an old toilet and a broken rocking chair. He'd followed Luther for several miles, and had seen him stop his truck over and over again to pick up rocks or salvage bricks. Max said he finally gave up when he saw Luther jump out to snap a tarpaulin over the back of his pickup, so the rocks wouldn't get wet in an upcoming thunderstorm.

Hank stopped laughing long enough to say, "Did you speak to him today, Emily?"

"Hell, no. I didn't want to get near him. He smells."

"He might smell, but that odor you smell is the scent of money. He's loaded."

"Are you serious? I thought it was his family that's loaded."

"Same thing," Hank said. "His father's dead now. Luther inherited everything from him and then some."

Luther's father, Arthur Summerfield, had been a successful trial lawyer. He had enjoyed a reputation as a womanizer too. This might have been a disadvantage in his law practice, but most people who knew him had no problem with his philandering: mainly because his deceased wife was originally from Charleston and everybody had hated her. "Run-down Charleston society bitch," was what people said about her. "White trash defense lawyer," was what many people said about him.

"Was Mr. Summerfield a sexual predator, Hank? That's what I've heard about him."

"I don't know. We didn't run in the same circles. I spent a lot of time at court with him, though. He was a good lawyer."

"He was still a womanizer," I said.

Hank didn't take the bait. He looked at me calmly and said, "Regardless of his sexual practices, Arthur Summerfield was well-known and respected in the Yemassee black community, Emily. He represented many of them at no charge, even when they didn't qualify for indigent defense."

"What about Mrs. Summerfield. Do you think she knew about his philandering?"

"I don't know. She was such a socialite, I doubt if she ever let anyone figure out what she knew and didn't know."

We didn't need to discuss Mrs. Summerfield any further. Luther's mother was a social butterfly and that was a strike against her. But there were even nastier aspects of her character: for one thing, she was an absolute and unrepentant racist. Marie and Adelle told me Mrs. Summerfield's maid had to drink water out of a paper cup, and use the bathroom outside or not at all.

We heard footsteps on the back porch and knew it was Max. He stomped the dirt off his feet on the door mat and came into the kitchen to join us. "What y'all talking about? Got a beer?"

"We're talking about Luther Summerfield," Hank said, "Emily ran into him today in town."

Max helped himself to a beer and sat down at the table. "That Luther's a piece of work, isn't he? He's the biggest momma's boy I've known. He still acts and thinks like a kid."

That was true: Luther's mother had adored him.

I was curious. "What does Luther do for a living?

Max and Hank laughed. "Luther doesn't even have a real job," Max said.

"He's never even applied for a real job," Hank echoed, "and he still lives in the house he grew up in. He didn't even move out when he married that one time. He stayed at home with his parents, and his wife stayed in town. Can you believe it, after his honeymoon was over Luther never spent a whole night with his wife; he went home to his momma and slept in his old bedroom. She cooked three meals a day for him, did his laundry, and loaned him money when he needed it."

Max laughed, "It isn't funny, but when Luther dies and they bury him next to his wife, they'll be closer in death than they ever were in life."

"Didn't he beat her up a couple of times?" I asked.

"Luther was in and out of jail for domestic abuse," Hank said, "but it didn't matter to his mother. She was on his side no matter what he did. She doted on him until the day she died."

"She was killed in that car wreck along with Luther's wife, wasn't she?" I said.

"Yeah. His son and daughter-in-law were injured in the wreck too," Max said. "They were here visiting when the wreck happened. They had only been married a few years and had one child." Max shook his head and pressed his lips together.

"They died at the hospital a few hours later and so did the driver of the other car. He was drunk."

I remembered that after it happened some folks said the accident was 'just rewards' for a lawyer. The drunk had no license and no insurance. There was no one to sue.

"I remember when that happened," I said. "I'm sorry they were killed. It must have been a terrible shock to Luther. How many years ago was the accident?" I asked.

"Probably three at the most," Hank said. "The sole survivor was Luther's grandchild. She was hospitalized for weeks afterward, but pulled through. She was only two years old when her parents died. I doubt she remembers them at all."

Max shook his head, then said, "Luther stayed by her side day and night until he brought her home. He and his father took care of her after that."

"I guess it's a good thing Luther didn't have a regular job. At least he could stay home with his granddaughter and collect junk part-time."

"Maybe he'll write a book someday on how to be a successful junk collector."

Hank laughed and then his smile disappeared. "We really shouldn't make fun of Luther. He doesn't have anybody in his family left now but the one granddaughter. And not only that, but after all she's been through—losing both her parents and her grandmother—I hear she's just been diagnosed with leukemia. God knows...Luther must be flat out devastated underneath that tough act."

That thought sobered me up. I know all about acting tough when you really wanted to run and hide. And so did my brother.

A delle appeared at the house early the next morning. She was wearing her signature sailor's hat, but her trademark pipe was nowhere in sight. I said, "It's windy this morning, Adelle. Might rain again. Where's your rain coat?"

She ignored me. "Miss Emily, you going over to Marie's today?"

"Yes I am, Adelle. Want to go with me?"

"Sho do. Ain't nobody hanging around too near Marie's house, so I can light up a few firecrackers."

"Oh, God, Adelle. Are you still lighting up those bombs?"

Adelle's grin gave me the answer.

"Since we're going to shoot off some firecrackers, let's stop along the road and pick some flowers for Marie's grave. I have some flower cutters in my bag."

"Okay. Just a minute," Adelle said. She was fidgeting with her pocketbook and seemed to be looking for something. "We're going to need some water. I'll meet you at the car. You driving?"

"Hell, no, Adelle. I can't drive with this cast on my leg. You've got to drive your car, or we'll have to borrow Max's."

"We'll take mine." Adelle disappeared into the back yard in the direction of the water hose, while I crept down the steps of the back porch and made it over to her car. It was a 1959 turquoise Plymouth Fury with mud flaps and curb feelers. The old straight-shift car was still in good condition, and its resemblance to the original TV Batmobile was uncanny even though it wasn't black. The seats had been re-covered in fun fur many years earlier and the floor and trunk were solid even though there were patches in a couple of places. I leaned against it to wait for Adelle. She appeared a few minutes later with the bucket full of water, and lifted the hood of the car. As she poured some water into the radiator, a large cloud of steam hissed out and I could smell the heat of the engine. Adelle closed the hood, placed the now half-full bucket on the floor board in the back seat, and got in the car.

"Hold on to that bucket, Miss Emily, don't you let it turn over."

I ignored her remark and said, "Let's take the back road today. Will your car last long enough to take the back road?"

She nodded and cranked up the car. I was surprised when it didn't backfire but one time.

"Adelle, there used to be a nice patch of daylilies in a ditch near the Brunson property. If they're still there we can cut some. If not, we can always cut Marie's lilies and take them by the gravesite on the way home. The flowers will be really fresh after that rain storm early this morning."

I then remembered Adelle's behavior at the funeral. "What did you put in Marie's casket, Adelle?"

"Nothing."

"Yes you did. I saw you."

Adelle was quiet. Her forehead wrinkled and she drew her eyebrows together. We had been driving, but now she pulled over to the side of the road and said, "I put a toothbrush and a mirror in there. The spirit needs those things just like a person do. If a spirit has 'em, it don't need to wander. It can rest." She paused again, then said, "Don't you tell nobody."

"I won't, but why...why did you put them in her casket?"

"The mirror will catch the light of her spirit and hold it down there if she tries to go wandering. The toothbrush is for her to use in case she gets out."

"Spirits don't use toothbrushes, Adelle."

"How you know? How you know? You don't know nothing about spirits," she said and pulled the car back onto the road. Her eyebrows were drawn together again and she adjusted her sailor hat, so I knew she was irritated.

When we reached the abandoned Brunson property, the daylilies were in full bloom.

"You cuttin' or you sittin'?" Adelle said.

"I'm cutting. What about you?"

"I'm sittin'. Don't you forget to throw something in that tall grass before you go in there. Snakes might be crawlin'."

I picked up a couple of bricks and threw them. When I didn't hear anything, I made my way through the grass to the blooms, cut them and filled the bucket full of daylilies. Then we headed to the cemetery.

The mound of earth above Marie's grave was still there. Although it had been lowered a bit from the rain, you could see it was a newly filled grave. Fresh flowers and plastic ones lay on top of it, along with small wooden crosses placed on top of the flowers. Since the service, someone had jammed a metal pipe into the earth on top of the grave. Adelle tapped the top of the pipe with her hand and said, "That's good. That's good."

"Good for what?" I asked.

"Good for speaking with Marie's spirit if we needs to." She leaned down and whispered a few words into the pipe.

I did the same, saying, "I love you, Marie."

A deep roll of thunder sounded, and we hurried back to the car. We were safely inside before the rain started coming down. It quit raining a few minutes before we reached Marie's driveway, but the wind was still blowing wildly.

***

The dirt backroad to Marie's house wandered through the rural countryside parallel to the highway for almost a mile before returning to the main road. When you were on the highway, you could see Marie's house across the corn field if you looked hard enough, but since we were on the backroad we couldn't see her house at all until we reached her driveway.

We noticed right away there were fresh tire marks in the damp ruts. The wind was still blowing, and branches slapped and scratched the side of the car where the driveway narrowed before ending at the front steps of Marie's house.

Her house was small, painted white except for the blue haint shutters. It faced south to catch the breeze. A couple of pink rose bushes were planted near the front porch, and a lone palmetto tree was growing out of the brick foundation on one side of the steps. The yard was littered with leaves from the rainstorm, and several flower pots were turned over on the porch. As we parked the car and got out, we saw that the door to Marie's house was standing wide open. "Don't go near that house," Adelle said urgently. She grabbed her bag, stepped out of the car and pulled from her pocket a smaller, tan bag that was tied together at the top with a red string. She opened it, took out what seemed to be dirt, and began chanting in the strange singing language that was Gullah. Every few feet she'd throw out a few pinches of the bag's contents, turn around three times, cross herself and kick up some dirt. I suspected she was spreading crushed mint leaves to keep the haints away: mint was one of her favorite herbs. When she had circled the house two times, she shot off a few firecrackers and returned to the car. Her face was grim.

"You can get out. Ain't nobody gonna bother us now."

I believed her.

"I'm going ahead of you," Adelle said. She walked up the

steps, looked around and then came back down to help me. I walked in the front door first, Adelle following. She gasped when she saw the mess inside. "Good Lord, what in the world? Who could do such a thing? We already cleaned this mess up once. Somebody's fooling with us." Marie's house was really wrecked this time. Tables were turned over. Pictures were pulled from the wall, glass and paper scattered everywhere. Two windows were open, and the wind had torn Marie's ancient lace curtains into shreds that kept slapping against each other as they continued to rip apart in the breeze.

"Oh, this is bad. Real bad. A boo daddy done been here for sure," Adelle said as she began to walk through the house. "A boo daddy who don't want nobody messing with Marie's stuff."

"Maybe it's not a boo daddy," I said as I placed a picture of Marie's mother back on the mantle. "Maybe it's a boo momma, Adelle."

"Ain't no boo momma. Ain't no boo momma. Boo mommas keep a clean house. They just mess up people's heads."

Adelle began talking in Gullah again and pulled out another small bag from her pocketbook. I headed to the kitchen. The doors to the kitchen cabinets were standing open and pots were strewn across the floor. The back door was standing open too. Someone had left in a hurry.

The bedroom was in even worse shape. Nothing was left intact. The mattress was ripped apart, dresser drawers were turned upside down, and Marie's jewelry box was empty, its contents spilled across the floor. Marie's old steamer trunk was no longer shut: stuff was hanging out of it and clothes were thrown around the floor.

But stranger than the confusion in the ransacked room

was the collection of dolls and other toys. Almost everything a little girl could wish or dream of was inside Marie's bedroom. There were doll clothes of every size and type. A ceramic tea set for dolls was set up on a small table in the corner; all the pieces were there except for the teapot which had fallen on the floor and broken. I reached into the steamer trunk and found a doctor kit along with several children's books and a doll bed. I walked over to her closet and opened the door. A toy high chair was turned over in the bottom along with a toy stove and refrigerator. I shut the door and looked back around the room at the dolls: there were Raggedy Ann dolls; Raggedy Andy dolls too. Arranged against one wall were a Betty Boop doll, Barbie and Ken dolls, and two Cabbage Patch babies. A Baby Tears doll was still in its box and lying in the corner.

"Adelle, don't touch anything. I'll call the Sheriff."

I pulled out my cell phone, dialed up Greg's office and asked to speak to him. Fortunately he was in, and agreed to send someone out right away to investigate the break in. "I might even come myself," he said.

It didn't take long for his deputies to get to us. Hampton County doesn't always have a lot going on in the daytime, so instead of being trigger-happy or itchy-fingered, most of the deputies liked to 'blow and glow' to the site of any reported crime. The lead deputy made so much noise we could see several cars pull off the highway as he passed them before turning into the drive to Marie's house. In addition, two other squad cars pulled in behind him, blue lights twirling and flashing, after hearing the excitement in his voice over the police radio band.

"You guys having a slow day" I asked as they got out of their cars.

"No, ma'am. Regular sort of day," one of them said. "You ladies better stay outside while we investigate."

They took statements from me and Adelle and dusted for fingerprints everywhere they could.

"Smells like gunfire," one deputy said to another.

I glanced over at Adelle to make sure there were no firecrackers sticking out of her pocket, but she looked the other way and lit her pipe.

We sat on the front porch for almost an hour while the deputies went about their work. We could still see cars passing on the highway over the rapidly growing corn stalks in the field.

"Miss Em, you ever hear corn grow?"

"Not in a long time, Adelle."

We squinted in the sun, watched the cars, and listened for the corn to grow, but the traffic from the highway drowned it out. After the same green truck passed by for the third time, I asked, "Isn't that Luther Summerfield, Adelle?"

"Where?"

"Out there on the highway." But before she could focus in on it, the truck had disappeared around the curve.

A few minutes later it reappeared.

"Look. There it is again. The green truck. Whose is it?"

"I don't know, Miss Emily. I don't know Mr. Luther's truck well enough to make it out from here."

I was sure it was Luther. No one else would have a truck dragging that low in the back—probably full of rocks and old bricks. He passed by two more times before he disappeared.

"I think that man's obsessed with you, Miss Emily."

"Don't make me throw up. I'd rather be involved with a snake-handling preacher," I answered. The thought of being around Luther on any level made me feel physically sick, and I grabbed a mint out of my bag to get rid of the taste of bile I imagined in my throat.

"He might be like his Daddy. Crazy about women," Adelle said. "That woman could be you." Adelle grinned widely. "Sure could be so. I heard his daddy would screw a snake, if he could catch one with its mouth open. Mr. Luther might be the same way."

I knew the conversation was going downhill, so I kept my mouth shut and rocked in my chair. Before Adelle could say anything else about sprucing up my love life, one of the deputies came out on the porch. "Either of you been out back?"

"I haven't."

"Me neither," said Adelle.

I gave her another stern look so she said, "Except for when I was checking around things when we first got here. Why you asking?"

He handed over a stack of paper held together with a rubber band. "You might want this. Don't know if it's important, but if it is, it shouldn't get rained on."

The deputy went back into the house and I removed the rubber band to look at the papers. They were damp, but not wet, so they hadn't been outside long.

"Stop. Don't be moving anything until I check it out." Adelle tried to grab the papers from my hand.

"Damn it, Adelle, there's nothing to check out. This is just…a stack of…" And then I saw what the papers were—copies of money orders made out to Marie's sister, Annie. I flipped through them. There were money orders for thousands and thousands of dollars.

"Lord have mercy, Marie done robbed a bank." Adelle began crossing herself and talking in Gullah again. The only words I could understand were "Marie cross obuh few days done gone and 'e yent study 'e head 'bout 'tiefin." *Marie had only been dead a few days and she wasn't thinking about stealing now.*

Just as the deputies were getting ready to leave, Greg drove up in his own car. He was not dressed in his traditional sheriff's uniform, but was wearing khaki pants, a plaid shirt, and loafers. He still has a great ass, I thought fleetingly.

"Any luck finding Charlie?" he said as he walked up to us.

"No luck at all. The last place Charlie worked, according to Max, was for Diana Ross and the Supremes. He said that was the last time Marie heard from him too, so we figured we'd start there."

"Sounds like a good idea to me. You busy for supper?"

Before I could answer, Adelle looked at Greg and said, "You ain't kin to those Summerfields is you?"

I wanted to stuff her mouth full of firecrackers. She knew the answer to her question. She had known Greg as long as I had known him. She was just deviling me.

"Nope. No kin to the Summerfields. If I were, I wouldn't be working as a sheriff, I'd be on the other side of the courthouse table. You want to go to supper, Emily? They're cooking steak at Big Dan's Country Club tonight."

"Sounds good to me, but Adelle has to take me home first. I'd like to change clothes."

"You look fine just as you are. Adelle, you go on home. I'll take care of Miss Emily."

"I'll just bet you will," Adelle shot back, and mumbled something else on the way to her car.

"See you in the morning, Adelle. Okay?" I called.

Adelle didn't answer. She got into her car, sat for a few seconds, then got out again and said, "Okay, but don't you go getting foolish tonight. It's the first week after the full moon and…" We couldn't hear the rest of her advice because she was back in her car cranking it up. This time it didn't backfire, but the engine cut off a couple of times before she had it running smoothly.

Greg and I sat on the porch and waited for the deputies to complete their investigation. Before they left, he went inside and talked with them for a few minutes.

I was anxious to go through the money orders but I didn't want to make my interest obvious, so I kept them hidden away.

I was nervous about going to dinner with Greg because I wasn't sure how I felt about him. We hadn't seen each other in a long while and I was surprised that, after all of the time that had passed, Greg and I were still so comfortable together. It seemed as if we had only been apart a few days instead of many years.

Greg and I first met in high school. He was a senior. I was a sophomore. It was love at first sight, and when he asked me out on a date I was thrilled. Everything was right with my world until I told my parents about the date.

"You're not going out with that boy. He's from the wrong side of the tracks."

"Please, mother. Tell me. Tell me where the wrong side of the tracks is in Yemassee?"

"You're not going. I won't hear of it. And don't you go asking your father for permission. His answer will be no too."

She was right. His answer was no. So, Greg and I began sneak dating. I would ask some other boy my parents approved of to pick me up and take me to The Shack, a drive-in restaurant in Beaufort, where I would meet Greg. At the end of the evening, our friend would meet us again and take me home. We managed to escape detection for several months until someone...I don't know who...squealed on us.

My parents were furious. They packed me up and shipped me off to Ashley Hall, a girls' boarding school in Charleston.

It was a big mistake on the part of my parents. While the educational opportunities were wonderful at Ashley Hall, the opportunities to sneak out and see Greg were even better.

We were together on every possible occasion. Drive-in theaters were our favorite spot; we climbed into the back seat of the car and made out for hours. He said he was a breast man and loved to fondle mine. It didn't do anything for me, but I let him do it just the same. Greg also wanted to "go all the way". I didn't...at first. By the time I decided I was ready to lose my virginity, it was too late. Greg had become resistant. He didn't seem interested any more. I didn't want to come right out and say, "Let's have sex," so I just tried to breathe heavier in hopes he would notice it. He didn't.

Finally, when I was a freshman in college—I was enrolled at Agnes Scott College in Atlanta by then—and visits with Greg had become fewer and far between, we parted ways. Not because we didn't love each other, but because he had bonked a student who was in the Nursing School at the Medical College of South Carolina in Charleston, and gotten her pregnant.

I was devastated. I couldn't breathe when he told me. I began to cry immediately.

"Who is she, Greg? How could you. Are you going to marry her?"

The answer he gave was one I didn't want to hear. I knew what he was going to say: he would do the honorable thing and marry her. No one could have cried more than I did that day, and no one could have looked as miserable as Greg Campbell. He was a beaten man. He was going to pay a dreadful price for a testosterone surge, and I was too. He was the first and last person I ever loved without reservation—and the last man I ever completely trusted.

Before we'd parted ways he told me her name. After that I had so much anger in my heart I was determined to find out what she looked like. I would gloat if she was a hag. I had high hopes that, since she was obviously a slut, she would have only a couple of front teeth, knock knees and hairy moles on her face.

When I finally got a glimpse of her, she wasn't a hag. I had driven into Charleston with a friend who was a nurse, and we waited in the hospital cafeteria until she came in to eat lunch. She wasn't ugly. In fact, she was very attractive. My heart broke into even smaller pieces.

This was about the same time Max came to work for us. He provided a willing ear to my misery until I quit coming home for good. The combination of my mother's criticism and seeing Greg and his bride together was too much for me to handle.

I dated a lot of people after that, but the relationships never seemed to be as sweet or as much fun. Greg had been my good friend as well as my sweetheart, and I missed him.

It took years for me to get over him. I tried losing my virginity to a running back from the University of North Carolina during Easter break. It didn't work; he was too drunk. When I finally did lose it, I was drunk. I don't even remember his name.

The sun was going down as the deputies and Greg walked back out onto the porch. Greg asked, "Do you have a key to the house, Emily?"

I gave the key to him, and he locked up as the deputies drove off. He helped me down the steps and into his car.

"Greg, I know it seems a little crazy, but I need to ride in the back of the car with this bum knee."

"No problem," he said and opened the back door.

We didn't have much to say while we were on the dirt road. There were a couple of deep holes filled with water in the ruts, and he carefully avoided them. Greg liked a clean car.

When we reached the highway he said, "This is the first time in many years that you've been in the back seat of my car, Emily."

I blushed before answering, "I could have been back here a long time ago if you hadn't run off with that slut."

He laughed. I wondered what people would think when they saw us together again.

We didn't have a long drive. Big Dan's Country Club sat just off Hwy. 17, near the Yemassee Railroad Station. It was a filling station and grocery store in the daytime, but turned into a steak house at night. I'd heard about it, but had never been there.

The filling station itself had been in business for about fifty years. It had two gasoline pumps outside—old ones. An ad for Dekalb-Pfizer Corn was nailed on the front of the store, beside another that advised young women to smoke Lucky Strikes.

Greg parked the car on the side of the building. Before

getting out, he reached back for my hand and held it. "Are you okay, Emily?"

"Yes I'm fine."

He pulled his hand away and got out of the car. My eyes filled with tears, but I wiped them away before he opened the back door and helped me out. He handed me the crutches and took my elbow to guide me over the uneven gravel in the parking lot.

When we entered the front door, a surly old man in a flannel shirt glanced up and said, "You got reservations, Sheriff?"

Greg nodded yes, and the man jerked his thumb over his shoulder to indicate we should head to the back of the store. We had to go around the counter that stood in the center of the room. It served as a bar at night and there were several other surly men sitting on stools. All of them were drinking beer, except for one whose head was down on the counter next to a half-empty bottle of Thunderbird wine. There were no women around.

Another man at the back of the room opened a door that led into a long, narrow hallway. There was a line of people at the other end, waiting to get into the next room.

It took about ten minutes for us to get to the front of the line. The cashier stood just inside another door, alongside a big burly fellow, obviously the bouncer. There was a lot of noise as we walked in, but after we were inside the door there was a moment of silence. The bouncer yelled out to the band, "Y'all play us a song, you hear?" The band members hurried to the stage and began playing "Blue Eyes Crying in the Rain." The lead singer took the mike and started singing in a high-toned nasal voice as if he were imitating Willie Nelson.

"Jesus," someone said, "I bet every cat in the county will be mating tonight when they hear this guy."

After Greg paid the cashier we were handed paper plates and utensils wrapped in paper napkins; they were printed with a favorite Lowcountry redneck slogan: *We don't give a damn how you did it up North.* Greg and the man in front of us engaged in a sort of conversation about nothing before we were directed to a long table filled with food. First, there was a large enamel pan full of greasy steaks. Next came bowls of potato salad, cole slaw and potato chips. A huge tray of baked potatoes wrapped in aluminum foil sat by the salads. There were slices of pound cake on the end of the table next to Styrofoam cups of ice. A young woman with a toothpick in her mouth was serving tea. She was wearing too much makeup and too little clothing. I wonder if she knows how ugly her navel is? I thought.

"Let's find a seat," Greg said. "I'll get you situated and then come back for our meal. There's no way you're going to manage those crutches and a paper plate full of food."

We edged our way through the crowd and I could feel the stares. Most people wouldn't remember who I was, but everyone knew who he was. I just hoped they knew he was divorced.

We found an unoccupied booth in the back corner. My knee was beginning to throb, so I lifted it up onto the chair next to mine. Greg went off to get our meal.

By the time he returned I had lost my appetite: Luther Summerfield was sitting across the room, and he was staring at me. He was dressed in normal clothes. Expensive clothes. Even so, he was still ugly.

"Greg," I said and took his arm, "Luther Summerfield is here."

"So?"

"He's staring at me."

"I don't blame him."

"No. You don't understand. It's more than that. He showed up at the courthouse on the day Marie's will was read. He kept driving by Marie's house today. He drove by over and over again. He must have passed by seven or eight times."

"There's no law against driving by someone's house, Emily."

"I know that, Greg. For God's sake, I know that. But how many times can a person ride by a house before it becomes intrusive?"

"As long as they're on the highway, there's nothing you can do about it. Luther has always been nosey. I'm sure he's just trying to figure out what's going on. Any reason he should be stalking you, Emily?"

"Of course not." My hand went instinctively to my bag where I had put the copies of the money orders. Was there a connection? Could Luther have been giving Marie money? Did Luther know something about Marie's death?

"Greg. They did find something strange today at Marie's."

"What?"

"A large stack of copies of money orders made out to her sister."

"I know. They found them lying outside by the back steps."

"I haven't added them up, Greg, but there are thousands of dollars. Thousands. Thousands and thousands and thousands of dollars."

"Emily, that's another thing there's no law against, having thousands of dollars." Greg said patiently. Maddeningly patient.

I pushed the hair back off my forehead and leaned across the table as best I could with a gimped-up knee. "Where in the hell would Marie get thousands and thousands of dollars? Where? You tell me, Greg. Where?"

Greg put down his fork. "Emily, I don't know where she got the money. I'm here with you, eating supper, and trying to have a good time. Take your mind off of Marie for a few minutes. Can't you leave it alone? Long enough for us to have supper?"

"I'll try."

"Tell you what. Why don't you ask her sister? Her home in Augusta isn't that far away. You can be there in two hours. If you can wait a few days, I'll take you."

"Okay. Thanks." I leaned back and looked across the room. Luther was gone. I sat up and looked all over the crowded room. He was nowhere to be seen.

"Are you going to eat, or do you prefer your steak cold?"

"Greg, I'm just not hungry. The steak is overdone and..."

"I didn't promise you the best steak in Yemassee. You're going to have to come out to my place one evening for that."

Tears welled up in my eyes again. "Greg. You know I've always loved you. You were my first love, but it's been too many years. I have a life of my own in Savannah. I'm only hanging out here to tie up the loose ends for Marie, and I can't drive. I CAN'T DRIVE. When it's over, I'M GOING HOME." I was shouting, and people at the tables near us were starting to stare. "I'm not coming back until my mother's dead—and I may not come back then."

"Jesus, Emily, I'm not asking you to marry me and I'm not asking you to move in with your mother. I'm just asking you to come over to dinner one night. Savannah isn't half way across the world, you know."

"Okay, Greg. I'm sorry. I'm just distressed over the mess at

Marie's house. I don't understand what's going on, and I know something is terribly wrong about her death."

We didn't have any further conversation on the way home, and Greg didn't kiss me good night at the door.

When I got to my bedroom, I was wide awake. The one martini I enjoyed at dinner hadn't made me sleepy, but it seemed to have heightened my senses. The money orders were still hidden in my bag, so I took them out, spread them on the bed, and sorted them by day, month and year. There was no logic to their sequence. I finally quit when I realized the amounts of money were random—sometimes hundreds of dollars and other times thousands of dollars. There was no regularity to the dates on them, either. I separated them into piles by year and got ready for bed. There was no hot water for some reason—the old water heater was finicky. I brushed my teeth, placed the stacks of money orders on the dresser, cut off the light and climbed into bed.

I couldn't sleep. The sounds of crickets were especially loud. The air conditioners weren't on—it was cool outside—but I was warm. A whippoorwill whistled, and I heard a dog barking in the distance. I listened for a response from Doodles, but there was none; he was probably with Max and soundly asleep.

I counted sheep and visualized them jumping over fences. It didn't work. I counted backwards from one hundred. One hundred—minus two—is ninety-eight, plus one is ninety-nine; minus two is ninety-seven and so on.

That exercise didn't work either. The crickets seemed be chirping louder and louder and louder. I stayed in the bed for a while longer, then cut on the light and sat up. I was wide awake.

I remembered that crickets could help you determine Fahrenheit, so I decided to try that. To figure the temperature, all one had to do was count the number of cricket chirps in a minute, divide by four and add 37 or 40, depending on whose theory you believed. I moved the table clock around so I could see the minute hand. When it reached the top I began counting the chirps. It was a futile exercise, but one I liked better than counting imaginary sheep in the dark. One...two...twenty... thirty-five...and, finally, eighty. There were eighty cricket chirps, so I knew it was fifty-seven or sixty degrees outside, give or take a degree or two in either direction. It was cool, yet I still felt over-heated. And still wide awake.

The stack of money orders sat on the dresser, and as I looked at them I noticed for the first time that several piles were considerably higher than others. I decided to total up the money orders for each year. I didn't have a notepad handy, so I crept along the hall and down the stairs to the kitchen to retrieve one.

When I reached the kitchen I opened the drawer under the phone, where my mother always kept something to write on, and grabbed the first pad up. Underneath was an old photograph of Jim and Zerelda. It had turned brown with age, but the images were still clear. Jim had on a rumpled pin-striped suit, and Zerelda wore a white dress and huge hat. She was taller than Jim, and skinny. It must have been taken close to the time she died, because she was very pregnant.

I stared at the picture and my mind raced back in time to 1954.

When we were growing up, Hank and I would usually be locked out of the house in the mornings to get fresh air and stretch our imaginations. We would wander over to the tenant section looking for amusement and entertainment.

Jim and Zerelda lived in a former slave cabin by the side of the road leading to our house. Jim had been born there to parents who were slaves.

The outside of the wooden cabin was weathered and gray, except for the boo daddy blue shutters and door, but the unvarnished heart-pine walls on the inside had a golden, yellow glow. Zerelda was proud of her home. "I likes it white glove clean," she'd say.

Outside, the cabin had a back yard surrounded by a hedge row. The hedge row along the side was all tangled up with honeysuckle vine, and so thick and full of wasps that nobody wanted to go near it. There was a hen house in the far corner, but the chickens were always getting loose and preferred to lay their eggs under the house. A couple of guinea hens ran loose too. There was a large stump with an axe stuck into it in the middle of the yard.

Directly behind the far side of the cabin was another large hedge row that hid an outhouse. The land then gently sloped down a bank to a secluded meadow with a small creek running through it. You couldn't tell what was behind the hedge row unless you went back there. The stream wasn't very deep, only two or three feet at the most, but it ran swiftly on its way to St. Helena Sound and the ocean.

Clumps of water willows grew along the creek. Hank

and I loved to sit there and watch the dragonflies dart back and forth. Zerelda said dragonflies were really snake doctors, and we shouldn't stay anywhere near them because they were looking for sick water moccasins.

Zerelda taught us to fish that spring when the bream were nesting. She showed us where to dig for worms, and we fashioned fishing poles out of sticks. We made hooks out of leftover wire from her clothesline, and tied them to our fishing pole with a piece of string. Lots of days we didn't even bother to tie the string and hook to a stick; we tied them to our fingers instead and jib fished above the bream beds along the bank.

We always gave any bream we caught to Zerelda. We couldn't take them home; we tried once, but our mother said we could only bring things into the house that looked like they came from the A&P.

We called this special area Daffodil Creek because every spring morning when the daffodils were in bloom, we would secretly pick the ones that lined the driveway to our house, and stick them in the wet sand along the side of the creek. Those daffodils lasted two or three days before drooping over and falling into the creek. Our mother's hysteria over the missing blooms usually lasted just about as long. By the time she put two and two together and figured out who was stealing the daffodils, we were grown.

Daffodil Creek was especially useful to Zerelda and Jim, because they didn't have any running water or indoor plumbing in their cabin. There was an old pump in the yard but when the days were warm they washed themselves and their clothes in the creek. If it was cold and the pump was frozen, Jim brought water from the creek up to the house; he also kept a rain barrel filled with water in case it was needed.

At some point in the past, Jim had put an old claw-foot

tub between the shack and the back hedge where no one could see it. The tub, raised up by four concrete blocks, sat over a dugout pit where he could start a small wood fire under it when anyone needed a warm bath. He used this same pit for cooking a pig: he and a friend just moved the tub over and sat a wire rack on top of the same concrete blocks and started a bigger fire for cooking.

Two clotheslines were attached to poles stuck on either side of the back hedge, positioned to run together in a v-shape about five or six yards behind the tub. Whenever Zerelda washed sheets, she took a long, hot soak in the tub and lay there enjoying the sun and the scent of the freshly laundered linens surrounding her in a sort of tent.

In cold weather they bathed in an old wash basin inside the house. Jim always kept the small fire going outside under the tub full of water just in case Zerelda wanted a nice warm bath.

Jim was already in his late eighties when I knew him as a child. Zerelda was much younger, some said as much as fifty years younger. She had been born in the South, but had moved up to New York City when she was still in her teens. Jim met her twenty years later on his one trip to the city. A friend had asked him to take a package to her. The next thing anyone knew, he had convinced her to marry him.

"Jim took one look at Zerelda and was bitten by the love bug," Marie used to say. "He refused to come home until she came with him." Marie also said she thought Jim had a potion mixed up to help him along with romance. "What's an old man 'gonna do with a young woman?" she'd say. "How long's he 'gonna keep her to himself?"

Adelle said someone gave Jim a potion of ground up cornflower blooms, and told him to put the dust in Zerelda's shoes. The powerful potion made a person fall in love with the one who put it in the shoe. "You gots to pick it in the spring when its fresh and you gots to dry it upside down or it won't grind up right," Adelle told me years later, "and once you puts it in somebody's shoes, they can't get away from you 'til you fix up a removing potion." Whatever Jim said or did, it worked. Zerelda came home with him.

Zerelda was pretty in an East African way, with bright hazel green eyes and light tan skin. She could pass for white at a distance. She was tall and slender, and her green eyes still danced that last spring. She had adapted back easily to rural ways and said she never missed living in the city. She wouldn't answer our questions about living with Yankees even though we pestered her daily with questions.

"Zerelda, do Yankees eat children?"

"Don't you go worrying about Yankees," she'd say to me, "you'll be much better off worrying about being happy." We didn't know what she meant by that, but she always gave us the same answer.

Zerelda never tired of our requests for information. She always listened carefully before she answered. We were especially curious about Chinaberry trees. The tree had beautiful blooms, but smelly fruit; there was one standing just outside the fence to their back yard.

"Zerelda, where do Chinaberries come from? Did the Chinese bring them here? Was it hard to bring a tree over the ocean?"

"Don't know where they came from," she'd say, "but they helps keep moths away in summer."

Zerelda rolled any winter clothing in the tree's leaves every spring and packed them away until they were needed again. She didn't use any moth balls.

Regardless of the poverty they lived in, Jim and Zerelda's clothes were always neat and carefully ironed. Their clothes may have been too long, too short or too big, but what they wore was clean and pressed. It seemed to me that Zerelda spent most of her time ironing. I eventually said, "Zerelda, is it hard to iron?"

She laughed as she handed the iron to me and said, "No, Missy. You can do it. You start on the back of the shirt." She taught me to iron that spring. "After you press the yoke on the back, you do one of the front sides. Then you press the rest of the back. Then you get to the other front side. Next the buttonhole and buttonholes strips. Then the cuffs and sleeves." The last piece pressed was the collar. "You need to have a straight-starched collar," she'd say, "You do it last." The irons rested on special plates that sat in the fireplace. When she took one out, she'd spit on it to make sure it was just the right temperature before pressing it to her clothes. "The iron sings a song, missy," she'd say, "and if you learn to recognize the right whistle when you spit on it, you'll never burn anything."

As I looked at the photograph, all of my senses seem to have been triggered at the same time. I closed my eyes. I could hear that whistle in my mind and the singing irons, feel the warm, moist air, smell the freshly starched shirts. And I could see Zerelda. Beautiful pregnant Zerelda standing there in front of the fire ironing, with the little beads of sweat rolling down between her swollen breasts.

One time I asked her, "Zerelda, why did you come back to the south?"

"I married Jim. I was so homesick," she'd said, "I would have married the devil himself. I'm lucky it was Jim that asked me home. He's an old man, but he's a good man."

Jim was a good man, that's for sure. He worked hard every

day doing any and everything that was asked of him. When he wasn't working, he was brushing Old Pet, his plow horse, or looking for horseshoes.

Jim collected horse shoes because he believed in their power. He nailed the horseshoes over all the entrances to his house for luck. He was forever stooped over collecting them. Marie said he hadn't always crept around all stooped over, but we found that hard to believe since we had never seen him stand straight up. Those horseshoes were central to Jim's life and beliefs. Zerelda on the other hand wasn't superstitious at all. "Jim's just an old man set in old ways," she'd say and then roll her eyes and look up at heaven when she heard him hammering up a new set. "Dear Lord, there he goes again," she said.

Marie always said Jim loved Zerelda more than he loved horseshoes. When I heard that, I knew they were really in love, because I knew how much the horseshoes meant to Jim.

***

Before our dad died, he had electricity put into the cabin. It was just for Jim—Zerelda was already dead by then. Jim was pleased, but he never used it to light up the cabin; he kept right on using the kerosene lamps that were a comfort to him. He did plug in an old radio our father gave him, and he would listen to it for hours. In the daytime it was anything he could find on it, but at night, when it got dark, he always tuned into WLAC's program—Nashville at Night. He showed us the best spot on the dial so we could tune in at night too. We learned to love the same rhythm and blues and gospel music that Jim was listening to.

This happened many years ago in the segregated South when we were young, but Jim shared a love of music with us that enriched us and changed our music preferences from then on. It was all gospel music on Sundays—songs like "Coming Up on the Rough Side of the Mountain" by the Rev. K.C. Barnes and the Rev. Janice Wells. We especially loved Sister Wynonna Carr and her song "Dragnet for Jesus."

Weeknights we listened to regular radio programming. Jim introduced us to Jimmy Reed, Lightnin' Hopkins, Muddy Waters, Little Junior Parker, Sonny Boy Williamson, Howlin' Wolf, and Etta James. We discovered Bobby Blue Bland and Johnny Shines on Chicago and Memphis radio. We learned the words to "Hound Dog" by Big Mama Thornton long before Elvis recorded it.

Along the way we also learned you had the blues if you woke up this morning with an ugly woman and your last hot check was gone. And you really had the blues if your old lady had a new man kicking in your stall. The idea of a man kicking in a stall in the barn was wildly funny to us even when we didn't understand it.

Whether it was the magic and soul of the blues, or the rhythm of the music, we were hooked on it from then on. We never did learn to appreciate Pat Boone.

We also grew up with something almost like fear of Yankees. One of the major reasons we were concerned was because Jim, who had been born in 1860 at the beginning of the Civil War, was scared to death of Yankee soldiers. He was constantly warning us to be on the lookout for them, even though we told him the war was over—that it had been over for years and years and years. But it didn't help: whenever he heard a car backfire or the sound of a gun firing in the distance, Jim would drop to his knees or hide behind something. He had been just a baby during the Civil War years, and whatever happened really made an impression on him. He never changed his mind about Yankee soldiers. Regular Yankees were okay, it was just the soldiers that scared him. He never told us why he was scared even though we asked him about it lots of times.

Jim eventually quit doing any real work around our place because of his age, but he still hitched up old Pet to the plow every day. He didn't grow anything, all he did was plow. When mother would complain that Jim was growing nothing but furrows, Dad said, "Leave him alone. Plowing every day beats pushing up daisies." I didn't know what that meant, but it shut our mother up.

Jim had a small pension from social security in his old age and our father continued to pay him wages, so he had no financial worries when he grew old. Jim died in 1960—two months before he turned 100. He was buried alongside Zerelda and the baby.

I put the picture of Jim and Zerelda back in the drawer.

My cell phone woke me up the next morning. It was Greg.

"Get out of that bed, Em. You still sleeping?"

"Hell, yes. I'm exhausted."

"Well, I have some information for you. I thought you were silly last night when you were talking about Luther, but here's something you need to know. One of my deputies came in this morning. Said Luther stopped him last night and asked all sorts of questions about you and Marie. He was especially curious about what you were doing in the house. Any reason why he would be nosing around like that?"

"No. No reason at all." Then I got mad. "I told you last night that he was nuts, but you didn't believe me."

"It's not that I didn't believe you, Emily. I thought you were over-reacting. I'm not as close to the situation as you are."

"Greg, I'm not close to it, I just don't understand why he would be interested in Marie at all. You know what a bigot he is. It doesn't make any sense, and I can't imagine any reason he would be concerned with me."

"I don't get the connection, either. You'd better go talk to Marie's sister as soon as you can; maybe she can explain it."

"I will, but in the meantime, can you find a way to track Charlie? I don't know where to begin. Hank's been looking, but he hasn't been having any luck either."

Greg agreed and went back to work. I hung my bad leg over the side of the tub and took a long leisurely bath before heading downstairs to breakfast.

Hank was seated at the kitchen table reading the morning

paper. He didn't look up when I came in, but said, "Any luck in your search for Charlie?"

"Are you making up a new cruelty joke? You know I haven't found a thing. How about you? Have you had any luck? I'm the one out here rummaging for information, and all you have to do is use the phone."

"Emily, have you ever tried to get the phone number of an entertainer? If you had, then you'd know how hard it is to break through the layers of celebrity bureaucracy." Hank was clearly irritated. "I've called Sony Records and MCA as well as most of the performance societies—ASCAP, BMI and SESAC. They said the best hope for finding a professional musician would be through the various local chapters of the Musicians' Union—anywhere he might have worked."

"Did they have Charlie Dixon listed anywhere in their records?"

"No. They said he wouldn't be listed unless he was a writer or publisher, but I thought it would be worth a try just-in-case." Hank got up and fixed a cup of coffee. He had a perplexed look on his face.

"What's the matter, Hank?" I could tell he was disturbed.

"Nothing, Em. I'm just tired, that's all." He leaned back in his chair. "I've done everything I can. Nothing's worked. Nobody's giving out any information at all, much less any phone numbers. Not even when I tell them I'm a lawyer. That really shuts them up. I can't even find out if Charlie Dixon was ever a member of anything at all." Hank shrugged his shoulders.

"What about the local chapters of the Musicians' Union? Did you try any of those?"

"Not yet. I have my secretary working on that. She's

contacting the unions in all the places Marie said Charlie worked…Detroit…Atlanta…New Orleans…Chicago."

"What about bigger cities?" I was hopeful for the first time that we might be getting closer to finding Charlie. "Is your secretary going to contact the unions in the main music centers? L.A.? New York? Nashville?"

"Of course." Hank looked at me like I was daft and I could see that he was irritated by my questions. "I'm running out of options. Why don't you try to find information about Charlie at the Golden Crab Supper Club on Hilton Head? The band plays on Saturday night—someone there might have a connection to Charlie. Call Greg and take him with you. You might get lucky. I've done just about all I can."

When I spoke with Greg later in the day, he offered to drive me to Hilton Head. It was a welcome offer; I was determined to find Charlie, and I wanted to spend time with Greg in spite of my resolve not to become romantically involved with him again. Ever.

"Let's leave early enough to see the sun set over Broad River," I said.

"You tell me when to pick you up, Emily. This is your show. But you know, if we go your route it'll take us longer to get there."

"I don't care. It's been a long time since I've crossed Broad River. It's so beautiful at sunset. You name the time. I don't care."

"Are you gonna meet me with your black drawers on?" Greg asked.

I laughed so hard I dropped the phone. "Meet Me With Your Black Drawers" On by Gloria Hardiman and The Professor's Blues Review was a popular Shag song. I hadn't heard it in years, but the title still made me laugh.

I picked the phone off the floor and said, "Stop it, Greg. Pick me up at six." I was still laughing so hard that I swallowed wrong and had a coughing spell. I had to sit down for a few minutes to catch my breath.

He arrived on time that evening. We passed the old Slave Cemetery on River Road where it dead-ended onto Hwy. 17—the main corridor between Savannah and Charleston.

Greg was fooling around with the dial on the radio, going up and down the FM band before changing to AM. He finally settled on an obscure rhythm and blues station that broadcast from a small strip center near Hilton Head.

"The signal isn't very good until sundown, Emily, but when it clears up, you're going to love the old tunes they play. It's pure beach, boogie and blues music."

He was right; I loved the music.

Just after we turned left on to Highway 21 at Garden's Corner we reached Bonnie's Produce. The slogan under its sign said, "A vegetarian's heaven." Sweetgrass baskets were hanging from the eaves of the store, and the tables outside were laden with early vegetables and fruit.

"Let's stop here for a minute, Greg. I'd like to see what's inside."

We stopped. Greg helped me out of the car and I checked out the vegetable tables before picking out four Florida oranges. There wasn't but one step up into the storefront, so he held my hand while I manipulated my crutch up the step to the antique glass sales counter. An attractive, elderly white woman sat behind it, and on the shelf behind her a huge black and white cat lay stretched out.

Before I could make a purchase, Greg said, "How big is that cat? He must be four feet long or more."

She laughed and said, "Oh, him? That's the Cookie

Monster. He showed up on my doorstep one night about a year ago and has never left. I think he's the biggest cat I've ever seen too. It's good luck when a cat chooses you. They say it makes you live longer."

I placed the oranges on the counter and noticed the sweetgrass baskets under the glass. Native Gullah-made baskets were a rarity now that people from all parts of the world had come to the Lowcountry and claimed Gullah kinship. A handsome oval basket with double handles sat on the bottom of the counter, and I pointed it out to the clerk. "How much is that basket?"

"Twenty-five dollars, plus tax." I found that hard to believe. A sweetgrass basket could now fetch anywhere from fifty to several hundred dollars and upward—far, far more than they used to cost.

"Twenty-five dollars? You must be kidding. Who made these baskets? Are they local?"

"No. They're not local. We import them from the Ivory Coast in Africa. That's where most of the slaves who came to this area can trace their ancestry. They brought the basket-making craft here with them."

I was flabbergasted. "You mean you can import authentic African sweetgrass baskets and sell them for less money than those made here in the Lowcountry?"

She shrugged her shoulders. "We used to sell the locally-made baskets, but they've gotten so expensive most of our clientele won't pay the price. One Gullah basket was placed in the Smithsonian a few years ago as an example of sweetgrass basketry, and now everybody reckons they're an artist."

She reached down under the counter and found a pack of Lucky Strikes. Taking a cigarette out, she tapped it on the counter before putting it in her mouth. "I can see paying good money for a basket sold at the market in Charleston, or by someone on Edisto or St. Helena Island—real Gullah people. But lots of baskets are being made by newcomers—African-Americans who've come here to make a quick buck. They've hijacked the culture, in my opinion. Hi-jacked it."

Greg took my elbow and said, "Let's go ahead and pay for your oranges. We can discuss sweetgrass baskets in the car. We don't want to miss the sunset."

He reached for his wallet before I could find the change purse in my bag.

"Greg, I'm paying for this. These are my oranges."

"No you're not. It's my treat. We'll take the basket my friend likes too," he added, turning to the clerk.

She took the still unlit cigarette out of her mouth and put it back in the pack. "I'm trying to quit," she said. Then she found a sales pad and added up our purchases.

As we left the store, I happened to glance up at a high shelf by the door. There were dozens of small bottles grouped there. I reached up for one and read, 'Fear Not Walk Over Evil Sprinkling Salt.' Next to it was '7 Sister Master Oil—a good mixture for dominating and controlling.' Yet another held a strange-looking mixture labeled 'Uncrossing/Jinx Removal.'

Then I saw the bottle of 'Run Devil Run' bath salts and burst out laughing. Greg saw me staring at the bottle and laughed too. He turned back to the clerk and said, "Did that come from Charleston?

"Nope. The potion store in Charleston closed up years ago. They say there's another one there now, but I don't know where it is. Savannah has a supplier too; I've heard it's somewhere in the historic district inside a hardware store. All of the stuff on that shelf came from Atlanta. Comes in handy every now and then. A friend of mine brought them to me. She's a big fan of Paul McCartney."

That did it for me. I rolled my eyes and said, "Let's go, Greg, before we get hexed."

After we were in the car, Greg said, "Emily, that wasn't a joke about Paul McCartney."

"How do you know?"

"Because I just bought his album *Run Devil Run*."

"Okay. You have his album. What's the connection?"

"Seems McCartney was in Atlanta to support his daughter's line of products at the Trade Show. He and his son wandered around downtown and stumbled on Miller's Rexall. It's an old-fashioned drugstore that caters to people who like spiritual, herbal and homeopathic remedies."

"You mean voodoo, don't you?"

"Not necessarily voodoo. It's a fine drugstore, but they do supply potions, roots, lodestones and other kinds of stuff to people all over the world. We haven't got a lock on black magic here, you know. They have all sorts of supplies there—Chinese herbal remedies, gypsy lodestones and crystals, South American and Caribbean potions, supplies from India. Lots of stuff from lots of places. You name it, they've probably got it. Nice folks too."

"You're kidding."

"No, I'm not. Check it out on the internet. Miller's Rexall has a web site."

"You think that's where Adelle gets her stuff?"

"I doubt it. Adelle deals mostly in white root voodoo—things that give people hope for better luck. She probably makes up her own potions or buys them somewhere in Charleston. Her cousin's a good resource for supplies: he's a powerful root doctor around these parts, especially north of the Broad River."

***

People who live in Beaufort County are always described as being 'north of broad' or 'south of broad.' South of broad usually means the person is a newcomer to the area and has an addiction to golf. North of broad generally describes people who have lived in the area for generations and would rather go to a cocktail party than play golf. Still others say 'north of broad' has an overabundance of strong women and momma's boys, and that 'south of broad' is full of tarted-up women and macho wannabees.

Regardless, the river that divides Beaufort County is considered by many to be one of the most beautiful sights in the region. This evening the Broad River was rough as usual. It never seemed to be calm even on still days with no wind.

The marsh along the river was streaked with the colors of sunset—pinks, purples, oranges, yellows, and gold. The same colors were sprinkled across the small waves on the water. Much of the marsh was still brown, with spikes of bright new growth rising above the old. By July, the marshes would be neon green, and each sunset would display even more psychedelic color intermingled with the cool gray water of the river as it rushed toward Port Royal Sound and the ocean beyond.

As we began to cross the mile-long bridge, fishermen were pulling their boats from the water at the public landing below the bridge. We rolled our windows down, and felt the cool air blow across our faces. I closed my eyes and inhaled the sharp smell of salt water.

There wasn't much traffic on the bridge. The sky was still shot with sunset colors, fading now, as we reached Lemon Island. Two egrets seemed to be frozen in position at the edge of the marsh on our left side; they were patiently waiting for a fish to pass by. A small roadside park on our right was empty but the trash can near the picnic table overflowed—remnants of the day's tourist traffic.

We crossed one more bridge as we left the last island patch. It was dusk, and the lights in the summer cabins along the shore of the small channel had begun to appear. On the dock closest to the bridge, a large brown pelican sat half asleep.

On the mainland, huge stands of pine trees shadowed the road for a couple of miles before the burgeoning Lowcountry development cut through the countryside, carving up the magic of the natural landscape into slices of commercial and residential sameness.

"Damn, Greg, look what's happened to this road. The beautiful overhang of the live oaks and moss is gone." I turned around and looked behind me. "Jesus, they've cut them all down and put in utility poles."

"It's all being developed," Greg said. "These new residents have to have utility service."

"I know, Greg, but the Lowcountry is being ruined. Where are these idiot developers coming from? Coney Island?"

"I don't know where they come from. Some are local, some aren't. I think they're trying to be sensitive to everybody's concerns—environmental and otherwise."

"The hell they are. If they were, they wouldn't call the subdivisions 'plantations'. They don't have any idea of what a plantation is and they don't understand or appreciate the beauty of the natural Lowcountry landscape. Look what they've done to the vegetation."

Greg didn't answer. Perhaps he was aware that the semi-tropical habitats that once served as a haven for birds and other wildlife now stood barren, stripped of their protective coats of grape vine, sea myrtle and gigantic spider webs.

When we turned on to the four-lane road to Hilton Head Island, the changes wrought by development seemed even more catastrophic to me. I wondered if Greg felt the same. I said, "Greg, do you ever miss the good old days...the days before Hilton Head was developed and everything changed?"

"Yep. Sure do. Although it's hard to remember that far back sometimes. Our zoning wasn't strict enough in the sixties. You've got nice residential areas right next to mobile homes and used car lots in some places."

"It may not have been strict enough, but our politicians have never had any problems raising taxes on the land. They raised taxes so high that lots of people—black and white— were forced off of their land."

Greg was silent for a moment, then said, "Beaufort County has prospered though; no one can deny that."

"I know, but it breaks my heart that so many of the Gullah people have lost their roots and moved elsewhere. The Yankees stole our land and gave it to the slaves, and now they've come back and stolen it from the descendants of slaves."

Greg shook his head and laughed half-heartedly, "Emily, that may be true, but look at the jobs that are available now because of the developments. The jobs wouldn't be here without these resorts."

I was angry. "Jobs? Is that a joke? Jobs? The only plentiful job opportunities for the children are as maids and janitors in the hotels and motels...cooks in the fast food industry or, if they're lucky, as caddies on the golf courses. Minimum wage jobs. How is that providing a better life?"

Greg shook his head. He was drumming his fingers on top of the steering wheel, so I knew he was irritated. "Emily, nothing can change what has happened here. Some good has come of it, though. It hasn't been all bad. The poverty level has lessened and the children aren't malnourished and full of parasites like they used to be."

"With no thanks to the developers. From what I hear, they didn't want any word out about the real condition of the islanders' land, or the health of the island children."

"True, but everything worked out in the end, didn't it?"

"I guess so. If uprooting a rich culture of people and replacing it with Saks Fifth Avenue and stores like that is what you call working things out. Let's not talk about it anymore." I looked out at the darkening sky and smoldered in a sullen rage for the next fifteen minutes.

It took us forty-five more minutes to get to the restaurant on Hilton Head. It was located on the far end of the island, in an older area that hadn't yet succumbed to the developers. The restaurant had been in business for a long time, and it was a favorite with everyone who knew about it. While it was advertised as a barbecue joint, you could order seafood, steak and chicken. Everything on the menu was consistently good.

There was a waiting list, so when the hostess offered us a hand buzzer, we took it and decided to pass the time in the bar. Since there were no open tables Greg pulled me along with him to order drinks.

"What'll you have, Emily?"

"Tell you what, I'm going to live dangerously tonight. I want a martini with lots of olives."

The bartender recognized Greg right away. "You here trying to put us out of business, Sheriff?"

"Not tonight, I'm here with a friend. We're looking for a man who used to live around these parts."

"Yeah? Who is he?" The bartender was making drinks, but his curiosity caused him to stay close to where we were standing.

"Nobody you'd know. We're looking for Charlie Dixon. He hasn't lived in the Lowcountry for years and years. Used to play in bands around here. You heard of him?"

The bartender shook his head no and pointed toward the end of the room. "That's the leader of the blues band over there. They're on a break. Why don't you ask him?"

Greg walked up to the band leader and had a short conversation before returning to our table. "Come on out to the hall, Emily, he says he'll call his friend in Los Angeles and see if he knows a Charlie Dixon."

My heart was thumping in my chest. I felt we were finally making headway in the search for Charlie as the band leader picked up the phone and dialed.

"Use my credit card," I said and handed it to him.

"Phone's busy," he said. "I'll try again in a minute. Tell me about this man, how'd you know him?"

"His mother just died, and we want to let him know she's passed—she worked for us a long time. We want to find him and tell him about her." I remembered my conversation with the woman at the hospital and added, "Charlie is a club player. We don't think he's a church player, but we're not sure."

"I know 'bout those club players. I'm one myself." He laughed and dialed the number again. When he got through he said, "Hey,'bro, what's Charlie's last name? That Charlie that you play with all the time? You know the one, plays the keyboards. I've got a lady here looking for a Charlie Dixon." He covered the mouthpiece with his hand, "How old is this Charlie?"

"He'd be around sixty or sixty-five, I think." I said.

"She says Charlie Dixon is around sixty. Sixty years old. Been gone from here a long time."

He held onto the phone and listened before handing the phone to me. "Here—you talk with him. He's gone to ask his buddies if they know a Charlie Dixon." He headed back to the band stand.

A few seconds later the man in L.A. was back on the line. "Don't nobody here know for sure what Charlie's last name was but it might have been Brown or Black, perhaps." He laughed wildly and hung up on me.

Oh, great, I thought. I wonder how many Charlie Browns

and Blacks there are in the United States? I finally realized the man was joking. I supposed he thought he was still talking to the band leader.

"They don't know Charlie Dixon, Greg."

"Well, I guess that means we've reached a dead end here, but there are plenty of other places to check. If you're going to Augusta, you might as well talk to some of James Brown's people. They know everybody in the music business."

Our buzzer went off, and we headed back to the lobby where the hostess led us to a table. The meal was delicious. Everyone in the room seemed to be having a wonderful time until the band leader stopped playing the blues long enough to thank the sheriff for coming in to enjoy the food and music. The room was noticeably quieter after that.

As we paid the bill and left our table, there seemed to be a mass exodus from the restaurant. Everyone must have finished their meals at the same time.

The parking lot was jammed. Greg helped me into the car and we sat for a few minutes waiting on the crowd to thin out. "I know you're disappointed, Emily. I don't know where else we can look."

I didn't answer right away. He knew from my face I was beginning to feel we were never going to find Charlie. "I am disappointed, Greg, and I'm frustrated too. Marie wanted me to find him. She said it was important."

"The funeral's over, Emily. Why don't you give it a rest for a week or two. There's no hurry now, is there?"

I shook my head 'no', but said, "I guess not, but something inside of me keeps pushing me to go on searching for him. I don't think I can stop until I find him."

Greg turned on the radio and leaned back in his seat. Now that the sun was down, the AM station was coming in clearly, with no static. The disc jockey was a good one and he knew his music. "Okay folks, we're going to listen to eight in a row. Eight of your golden oldie rhythm and blues favorites. Sit back, relax and enjoy yourselves. If you want to hear a particular tune, give us a call. Or drop by. We're here to play that special song for you."

The song series began with Otis Redding's version of "These Arms of Mine." Then came Aretha Franklin and "What a Difference a Day Makes." We listened to the music without speaking until we were approaching the 170 exit.

"Do you want to go back on I-95 or back across Broad River?"

"Doesn't matter." I was transfixed by the night, the moon, and the hypnotic music on the radio.

"Okay, we'll go back the way we came." Greg exited the Hilton Head Parkway onto Hwy. 170. We had only driven a couple of miles when the disc jockey announced, "Now, folks, here comes another Otis Redding hit that you're bound to remember if you were young and in love in the sixties. "If you've been loving too long to stop now..."

Greg slowed down and pulled off the road into the strip center where the radio station was situated. He parked in front of the large plate glass window; I could see the disc jockey inside, with his carts of music and microphone. The studio was dimly lit, and very little light spilled out onto the parking lot.

Greg turned up the radio very loud, got out of the car, and came around to my side to open the door. "Come on Emily, let's dance."

"I can't Greg, I have this bum knee, remember?"

"Doesn't matter. Get out and we'll just move with the music." He took my hand, and I stepped out into his arms.

We stood there, moving back and forth with the music until the song ended. We could hear the disc jockey describing the scene in the parking lot to his audience: "You're not going to believe the romantic sight out here tonight, folks. A couple just pulled up and they're dancing to the music of the great Otis Redding. What a special moment. You guys in the parking lot, don't ever lose what you have."

Greg reached down, pushed the hair off my face, and caressed my cheek. I wanted to lean harder against his shoulder, let him envelop me in the safety of his arms, but I turned away. I felt drawn to him, but I was afraid. I held onto the side of the car and sat down on the back seat. Until this moment, I had forgotten how romantic he could be. I was full of emotion, and I didn't know how to deal with it; so I didn't. I closed the car door before Greg could see my tears. My mother would have been proud of me.

Greg stood outside for several minutes before walking around to the driver's side of the car. He got in and we continued our drive home. We didn't say anything else to each other. Nor did he hold my hand again. Whatever we had felt in that special moment in the parking lot had disappeared. Our trip down that old lover's lane had ended.

A few days later I had a doctor's appointment in Savannah to check on the progress of my knee, and I'd forgotten to remind Max that I needed a ride. I put on a robe and went downstairs to explore my travel options. It was quiet and seemed as if everyone had already left the house. It looked as if I was going to have to break down and ask my mother for a favor.

There was a pot of coffee on the kitchen counter, still half full. I took a mug out of the cabinet by the sink and poured myself a cup. I didn't add any cream or sugar; I needed a heavy dose of caffeine to jolt myself awake and figure out how I was going to get to Savannah.

Little had changed in the kitchen since I was a child. While the old fireplace had been converted to a double oven, the portable dishwasher still stood under the window closest to the sink. There was a newer table in the center of the room, and the pantry had a new door. Otherwise nothing had changed. If you grew up in Yemassee and you'd learned anything, it was that white is the preferred color for woodwork, napkins, towels and sheets, and every damned thing in the kitchen. The refrigerator was white. The cabinets were white. The counter top was white. The linoleum floor was white. The tile above the stainless steel sink was white. The woodwork was white. There was no color in the room except for the purple African violets blooming on the shelf under the window. And they were planted in white pots. Anyone who used pastel or dramatic colors on any of those items was probably from a suspicious background—probably California. Or worse, a Yankee.

My stomach gave a huge growl, and I knew it was time

for a piece of toast or a bagel. The pantry looked promising, so I decided to forage for my breakfast. I found an unopened package of cinnamon-raisin bagels and walked back into the kitchen.

Suddenly a loud voice called out, "Good morning, Miss Emily,"

"Jesus, Adelle, you scared me to death. Where did you come from?"

"Where did I come from? I come from my house. That's where. I'm supposed to do the laundry for your momma today."

It was serendipity. Adelle was at the house and I could catch a ride to Savannah. "Adelle, is your car running okay?"

"Course it is. Why you ask?"

"I need a ride to the doctor. I have an eleven o'clock appointment in Savannah."

"I'll take you, but you buying the gas."

"No problem, Adelle. I'll buy the gas. You go ahead and start a load of clothes. I need to clean up. I won't be long."

Adelle shook her head and began mumbling as she walked into the laundry room. I went upstairs for a quick shower.

It was a warm morning, so I decided to wear a skirt and short-sleeved matching sweater. I put a sandal on my good foot. I put the other sandal in my pocketbook, in the hope the doctor was going to let me start walking early. I didn't put on stockings. Too much trouble, and too warm anyway.

Adelle was ready to go when I returned to the kitchen. "You better put some lightning fast on your feet," she said, "'cause you go be late if we don't hurry."

I hurried.

Adelle's car cranked up with no backfiring and we made it to the doctor's office on time. It was a good day for me. He removed the immobilizer cast from my leg and put an athletic wrap on my knee instead. "Take the immobilizer with you," he said. "If your knee starts bothering you, we can put another one on." He also advised me to continue using the crutches for the time being. "No driving for three more weeks," he said.

On the way home, Adelle was quiet. It was unlike her to keep her mouth shut, so I said, "What's wrong, Adelle?"

"Nothing. Ain't nothing wrong. I just got a lot to do when I get home. I got to do those clothes and I got to arbitrate with your momma."

"Arbitrate with my mother? What do you mean?"

"She say she wants me to work every day and take over where Marie done left off. If I do it, it'll mess up my on-the-side business."

I knew her 'on-the-side business' meant her voodoo practice, so I said, "Adelle, just tell mother you can't work but so many hours a day. You can set new hours for your customers. Mother is going to need a lot of help now that Marie's gone."

"She need help all right. E won col homny ooman."

"She's what?"

"E won col homny ooman."

"Speak English, Adelle, I can't understand you." Adelle had lapsed into the Gullah language in describing my mother. When she was talking to white folks, she talked in what we called normal English. When she was talking to customers and friends, she talked Gullah.

She glared at me and said very slowly: "She is a cold... hominy...woman. A...cold...hominy...woman."

I started laughing. Now I knew exactly what she meant. A cold hominy woman was one who didn't take care of her loved ones, but was fixated on herself.

"You're right, Adelle. I guess you could call my mother a cold hominy woman."

"If you ain't careful, you're gonna to be just like her."

Her remark surprised me. "Adelle. Why in the world would you say that? I'm not ever going to be like that way. I'm not a cold person. I'm not."

"Oh, you ain't? Then why you so stand offish with folks who love you? How come you stay by yourself all the time? How come you got your feet all stuck down in Savannah? How come somebody has to die to get you back up here—up here in Yemassee where you belongs?"

"Damn, Adelle. You're mean as hell today." I didn't say anything more than that. My relationship problems were none of her business. She had touched on a subject I didn't want to address, with her or anyone else.

We were home by late afternoon. The cold hominy woman was still out, so Adelle went back to doing laundry and I went to my room to take a nap.

everal hours later Hank woke me up with a knock on my bedroom door. "Emily, are you going to sleep all evening, or are you coming down for supper?"

I mumbled something and sat on the side of the bed, rubbing the sleep from my eyes before going into the bathroom to wash my face. My cell phone had fallen on the floor, so I reached down to pick it up and check it for messages, although I had not heard it ring.

There were no messages. The battery was dead. I had forgotten to recharge it.

It was a warm evening, and the air in the room seemed stagnant. I pushed the windows up, but instead of experiencing a fresh rush of spring air, I shivered and had a juju feeling something was out of whack and I didn't know what it was. I was filled with a growing sense of dread. I found an old sweater in the closet and put it over my shoulders before going downstairs.

My crutches were leaning against the wall by the side of the door, but I left them there. I figured it was time to begin using my leg a little. I took the cell phone downstairs to the kitchen, found the recharger and plugged it in. It rang immediately.

Hank and Max were both in the kitchen. "Greg's looking for you," they said, almost in chorus.

I rolled my eyes upward and answered the phone.

"Emily? Where in the hell have you been? I've been chasing you down all evening," Greg said.

"Well, you've caught me. What's up?"

"We've arrested Luther Summerfield."

"You've arrested Luther Summerfield?"

"Yes. This afternoon."

"Okay. Tell me. Why did you arrest him?"

"We had a fingerprint match from the ones we dusted at Marie's house. We picked him up for questioning, and he admitted being there."

I knew somehow that Greg wasn't telling me everything. "Greg, there's more to this than his breaking into her house, isn't there."

Hank and Max stood up and walked over to the counter beside me. "What's he saying?" Hank whispered.

I covered the speaker with my hand and said, "Shh-h-h-h-h."

Greg still hadn't answered my question. "There's more than a burglary, isn't there, Greg," I said again.

The clock began to chime. Bong. Bong. Bong. Eight times it chimed. There was silence on the other end of the line. Doodles had been sleeping on a blanket by the door and growled at the clock.

"Greg, damn it, what in the hell is going on?"

He finally answered, "We're not sure, Emily. I'm not in a position to share any other information with you tonight. Luther has an attorney. After we see a judge in the morning I may be able to discuss it with you."

"You can't discuss it with me? You can't discuss it with me?" I was screaming into the telephone.

"Emily, I'll talk with you tomorrow, good bye." Greg hung up the phone before I could yell at him again.

Hank and Max were staring at me. Their looks told me that I had better tell them what had been said, and I'd better tell them quickly.

"They found Luther's fingerprints in Marie's house.

They've arrested him. There's more to the story, but Greg can't discuss it."

"Greg can't discuss it?" Max said.

"Greg won't...will not...won't discuss it," I said and slammed my fist against the counter.

Hank's lawyer ego took over. "Cut it out, Emily." He was jabbing his finger toward me. "Greg can't discuss it. He can't discuss it because Luther has only been...accused...accused... of a crime. No reputable law enforcement officer should share details about a case before a perp is arraigned."

"Get off of your legal high horse, Hank. I don't give a shit about Luther's rights." I hit the counter with my fist again. "It doesn't matter, because Greg knows Luther's been stalking me. He knows I'm afraid of Luther, and now he knows Luther was in Marie's house. For all we know, Luther may have killed Marie." I was shouting at Hank now.

"Luther didn't kill Marie," Hank yelled back at me, "she died of a heart attack. I spoke to the coroner myself. Marie died of a heart attack."

I was really mad at my brother now, and got up right in his face. "Then he scared her to death. I bet he scared her to death." I was standing on tiptoes.

Max interrupted us, "Y'all better quit yelling or your mother is going to come down to see what's wrong and there'll be hell to pay."

That's all it took to shut us up. We shared guilty looks and sat down at the table.

"What's for supper?" Max said.

"Crow," Hank answered.

"Crow? Why would you say that, Hank?" I said.

"Because you were right all along. There surely is something going on with Luther. I just never imagined he would break into anybody's house. I can't imagine he would want anything that belonged to Marie."

Max said, "She didn't have much to steal. From what I saw, the only things anyone'd want to steal would've been her dolls. And only a kid would do something like that. A grown man—even Luther—wouldn't steal a bunch of play dolls."

"Hank. Max. There's something else you need to know," I said.

Both men stared at me. Max opened a beer, and I waited until its fizz settled down before saying, "Marie had a lot of money."

"Money? Marie? Marie had money?" Hank was incredulous.

Max just stared at the table before looking up. "What kind of money? What do you mean about a lot of money?"

"When we were at her house the other day, the deputies found a pile of money order copies dropped outside the door to her house after someone—I guess Luther—broke into it the second time. I haven't added it up, but it's really a lot of money."

Hank was silent. Max, too.

"All of the money orders were made out to Marie's sister Annie."

"God almighty, Emily, why didn't you tell me this before?" Hank said.

I was irritated. "I didn't tell you because you haven't been here. You've been staying in Charleston the last few days, remember?"

Max went to the refrigerator and opened another beer before saying, "Well, I've got a little information too."

Hank and I turned to him, expecting to see his usual grin, but it wasn't there. Max was serious. "I talked with Luther a few days ago."

"You talked with him?"

"Shut up, Emily, don't interrupt him."

"I talked with Luther after you told me you saw him in town and again at Big Dan's Supper Club. Ran into him at the hardware store. He was sitting in a chair by the old pot-bellied stove there in the middle. Nobody else was around that time of day, so I sat down beside him and struck up a conversation."

Max paused and flicked some unseen dirt off the knee of his pants. He had taken off his boots before entering the house, and his sock-clad feet were propped up on the chair next to him. "I don't know why Luther broke into Marie's house, but I do know this: Luther's grandchild is dying, and Luther is a desperate man. The little girl has leukemia and needs a bone marrow transplant. She also has a rare blood type with a lack of some sort of antigens. There are no matches with any relatives, and no matches with anyone in any of the donor pools. She only has a short time left if a match can't be found."

"That's really sad, Max, but what does it have to do with Marie?"

"Don't know that it does. I just wanted you to know that Luther may be losing his granddaughter. The man lost his daddy just before Marie died, and there are no more relatives living. I don't need to remind you about the death of his mother and son. You know how close he was to that wacky mother of his."

It was a sobering thought. Luther had lost all of his loved ones, except the grandchild. Some of his erratic behavior could be explained by this situation—but not all of it.

"Max, that's the same logic prison guards use in New Hampshire when they watch 'life without parole' prisoners make the 'Live free or die' license plates. You want me to think good thoughts about Luther while knowing I hate his guts."

The screen door had been left open. I walked over and slammed it shut, scaring poor Doodles out of his sleep by the door. He gave a yelp and ran over to Max for comfort, leapt up onto his lap and sat there shivering.

"You want me to put Doodles back down so you can kick him?" Max was disgusted with my behavior. He held Doodles close, calming him before setting him back down on the floor.

"I didn't mean to scare him, Max. I just get aggravated when y'all are sympathetic to that no-good son-of-a-bitch."

I picked up a couple of slices of bread and a jar of mayonnaise. "Any tomatoes around?"

"Check in the fridge," Hank said.

Max got up and said, "I'll do it. I need another beer."

"Any more beer and you're going to pass out," I said, but Max ignored me, fetched a can out of the fridge and handed me a very ripe tomato.

"Know the only thing that's better than a tomato sandwich, Max?" I said.

"Nope, what?

"Another tomato sandwich," Hank said quickly before I could.

We laughed together and ate our supper. We didn't discuss Luther until after we were finished eating.

"I'll clear the table and put up the food," Hank said, "if you'll wash the dishes."

"Okay. I'll wash, but you need to perk some coffee."

When I'd finished the dishes we all sat back at the table. Max was still drinking beer.

"When did Luther's father die, Max?" I asked.

"A few weeks ago."

"How close to Marie's death?"

"Dunno. Pretty close. Seems to me his memorial service was held a couple of weeks before Marie's funeral. Why?"

"Because I'm wondering if there is a connection with Luther breaking into Marie's house and his father's death."

Hank's eyebrows shot up. "Emily, you're nuts. Or Luther's nuts. Why, in God's name, would a man break into somebody's house because his daddy was dead? I don't think Luther plays with dolls."

"Jesus, Hank. I was just asking a question. What do you think, Max?"

Max scratched his head and said, "I can't think of a connection, but who knows. I'll ask him. I'll go down to the jail in the morning and ask him."

"He'll be out of jail before morning," Hank said. "The Summerfield law firm will be crawling all over the sheriff before the sun comes up. Hell, they might have Luther out of jail tonight."

"Don't you have to have a bond hearing?" I asked.

Hank just laughed and said, "Yep. You sure do—unless you're a member of a privileged class and you can call in a favor from a judge."

Max yawned and stretched his arms out. "I'm headed home. Come on, Doodles. Bedtime."

The door slammed shut. "Damn spring on that door's too tight," we heard him mutter as he left.

Hank and I straightened up the kitchen and he went back to Charleston.

It was just before lunch the next day when Max came back to the house. I was still in bed, and he called up the steps for me to come down. I threw on a robe and headed to the kitchen.

Max started talking as soon as I walked through the door. "Here's the scoop. Luther's father left a lot of money to Marie in his will. That was upsetting enough to Luther, but he really got mad when he started going through the books and found out how many thousands of dollars his father had paid to Marie over the years. What he said was he just lost it, and had to drive over to Marie's to ask her about the money."

"Did he kill her?"

"He said he didn't touch her. Said she threatened him and told him to get out. Said she just got furious. Called him all sorts of names. Told him he didn't have any business being there."

"He didn't, Max."

"I know that, Emily, but he thinks he had a right to be there and ask her about the money." Max leaned over toward me, lowered his voice and said, "And Luther has no idea about the copies of money orders and the thousands of dollars sent to Annie. That money must have come from his father too."

"Was Luther there when she died?"

"He wouldn't say."

"He wouldn't say?"

"Nope. He closed up like an oyster when I asked him about her death."

"Then he must be guilty. The son of a bitch. I hope he rots in jail for breaking into her house."

"He said he didn't break in. He said she opened the door and let him in."

The phone rang. I jumped up to answer it and almost tripped over the chair, but steadied myself in time. The phone quit ringing before I could answer it.

"Well, Max, I guess this fills in the missing blank. We know who was giving Marie money. Now we need to figure out why." I sat down and looked at him.

"Emily, there's more."

"There's more?"

Max stood up and walked around the room. He stared out of the window above the sink. Then he swallowed a couple of times and said, "Luther said his daddy sort of made a deathbed confession."

"He did what?"

"Mr. Summerfield was dying. Both Luther and his dad were upset about the grandchild's leukemia. They knew time was running out for her because a match to her blood type can't be found. You know, blood with the same lack of antigens. "

"So?"

"So Mr. Summerfield said he had another son. Said Luther had a brother. A half-brother that was born to a black woman."

I was stunned. My throat dried up and I couldn't speak. I hobbled to the refrigerator for a bottle of water and drank it. I was too troubled to say anything.

"You okay with this, Emily? I'm telling you this because I think it may help us understand what the hell has happened around here lately."

"I'm okay, Max. I'm just shocked Marie would have an affair with old man Summerfield. He was such a sleaze ball."

"Well, maybe now you can understand why Luther may have been a little shocked himself. That was the bad news."

"The bad news?"

"Yep. The bad news was that Luther had a black brother. Looking at it another way—the good news was that this brother could be a bone marrow donor match for his grandchild—if he could find him."

"Max, I can't believe this. He thinks Charlie is his brother? Charlie? Our Charlie?"

"Hell, Emily. He doesn't know. His father died before he could tell him who the woman was—just like in the movies. Luther said he didn't have any idea where to start looking until his father's will was read. He was certain it was Charlie when he found the records of those cancelled checks made out to Marie."

Max had an annoying habit of scratching inside his ear when he was about to deliver bad news. He had scratched several times earlier, and I knew a real humdinger was headed my way.

"Emily, Luther said Marie wouldn't tell him anything about Charlie. She told him she would dance with the devil before she let him get his hands on Charlie or any of her kin and..." Max shifted feet and scratched his ear again. "...she said she didn't have much time left and wasn't going to spend it helping him."

"What did she mean she didn't have much time left?"

"I guess she knew she was going to die soon. I don't know. She was in her nineties and she had a bad heart, so she knew her time was coming."

He paused again and said, "Luther admitted he trashed Marie's house—both times. He said he was looking for information on Charlie. He didn't find anything."

"Damn. Now I know why Luther kept following me. He's scared I'm going to stumble onto the fact Charlie is his brother."

"Odd, isn't it? Luther has always been such a racist, and now the person that may save his grandchild could be a black man. What a twist of fate."

It was hard to believe. Charlie's father could be Mr. Summerfield. If this was true, then Marie'd had a complicated and serious relationship over the years with a man she professed to despise. It now made sense why she always managed to disappear when any of the Summerfields were around.

After Max left, I walked into the laundry room to get some clean underwear. Adelle was sitting in the rocker in the corner staring out of the window. She wasn't her usual jovial self. Her eyes were sad and she was rocking from side to side. Before I could say anything to her, she said, "I heard what you was talking about. Marie ain't messed with that Summerfield man."

"Adelle, how do you know Mr. Summerfield isn't Charlie's father?"

"I 'jes know, that's why. Marie's husband Amos was Charlie's father. I knowed Marie all these years and I would've known if she'd been foolin' around with a white man."

It was no use to argue the subject with Adelle, I knew that. She was deeply disturbed with the turn of events; and I was too.

"Tell you what, Adelle, I'm going over to the old cabin later today to check on things. Why don't you come with me?"

"No, ma'am. I think I'll stay here." She wasn't budging.

"Come on, Adelle. Keep me company. Please?"

"I said no and I means no. I ain't going. I got work to do for your momma, and I got gout in my toe too."

That was it. I was going to the cabin by myself. I was curious about the condition of old cabin, but I was even more curious as to why Marie had been over there so many times before her death. Maybe the secret to Charlie lay in her visit there.

efore leaving the house, I put on an old pair of jeans and boots. The no-see-ums were out, so I covered myself in Avon's 'Skin so Soft' to keep them away. I also tucked a couple of sheets of fabric softener inside my bra and the pockets of my jeans too, in case the skin softener didn't work. Both products were well-known mosquito repellents. I'd already put my cell phone in my bra. I decided not to take the crutches: my knee felt fine, and I was sure a little exercise would do me good in spite of the doctor's warning to be cautious.

It wasn't a long walk to the cabin. The original path through the pecan grove had disappeared with time, but I remembered clearly where it once was. The bees and wasps were out in full force, taking advantage of the yellow and white honeysuckle vines blooming along the side of the pasture: the air was heavy with their fragrance. I could taste the honey in my mind, and I reached over and selected a yellow bloom to suck out the nectar. Its taste was just as sweet as I remembered. There were clumps of high grass along the edges of the old path. You never knew when a snake might be lurking about, so I picked up a small limb and made a lot of noise.

Half way to the cabin, I noticed the old fence behind Jim and Zerelda's house was gone. A few posts stuck up at haphazard heights. The ancient outhouse was there in the back, only now it was covered with honeysuckle vine too. The rusty hand water pump was still just visible among the grass and weeds, but its handle had fallen off.

Every now and then I would hear a car or truck going down the road. I couldn't tell which because the hedge in front of the cabin had grown so tall over the years the highway was hidden.

When I reached the back of the cabin I looked around the yard; and there sat the old claw-foot tub. It lay on its side, the bottom rusted out. I thought about how much Zerelda had loved that tub. I also thought about the day Zerelda and the baby died. I remembered how hard Hank and I had run to find Marie.

The sound of a truck going by interrupted my thoughts before fading away into the distance. I looked up at the cabin, and it seemed as if nothing—yet everything—had changed over the years. The only parts of its weathered wood that had ever been painted were the shutters and the front door. They had once been a bright blue. "Blue keeps the haints and boo daddies out," Jim used to say. Now they were faded to the color of pale blue chalk.

The cabin had two entrances: one at the front that was always closed and another at the side, opening into the kitchen. The windows were intact, but most of them were cracked. A few panes were missing altogether.

Jim's horseshoes were nailed all over the top and along the sides of the back door. I smiled because I knew most of the shoes had come from Old Pet, the plow horse he loved. Something looked peculiar, though. I stepped back and looked at the collection of horseshoes again.

"Oh, my God," I said out loud. "All of the horseshoes are hung upside down. No wonder Jim had such bad luck. He let all the luck run out of them." A vision of Jim, Zerelda and the dead baby sprang into my mind. I could almost feel their presence. Tears stung my eyes and I rubbed them with the knuckle on my index finger. This made things worse, because the skin softener got into my eyes and really made a mess of it. I sat down on the back steps and blinked for what seemed like a hundred times, dabbing at my eyes with a Kleenex. When the tears finally dried up, I went into the cabin.

The kitchen floor was made of wooden planks, and I could see the ground underneath where the knotholes had fallen out. As I watched, a field mouse scurried across the floor and disappeared through one of the holes. There was a shelf running along the whole right-hand side of the room, and an ancient pie safe sat on the left side. I was surprised no one had stolen it. There was still an icebox to the right. I remembered when Jim had painted the icebox bright red—red was Zerelda's favorite color. Hank and I helped him paint it, and we were in plenty of trouble when we went back home with oil paint all over our clothes. We didn't care. We were used to getting spankings—it was the price we paid for having fun.

The old red icebox also brought back the memory of sneaking over to the cabin on summer days when the ice wagon arrived. Zerelda would grab an ice pick and chip pieces of ice off the new block. As it began to thaw, she'd stick slivers of ice in sugar for Hank and me. We had to stay inside while we ate them because there were too many bees and yellow jackets waiting outside: they loved sugar too.

The dust in the kitchen had settled from the moisture in the air, but it still made me sneeze. I took out a Kleenex and blew my nose before walking over to the black stove at the far end of the room. I noticed that a box to its side was still full of kindling wood. There were a few pieces of coal, too.

The room seemed so very cold to me. It was cold just like the day Zerelda died. A floorboard creaked as I stepped through the door from the kitchen to the living room. I looked around. There was a fireplace on one end, and a dark green sofa on the other. The irons that used to sit on the hearth were gone, but a large black pot hung inside the fireplace. A straight chair was set against one wall and an old wooden rocking chair against the other. Although the cabin had electricity, there were a couple of kerosene lamps hanging from hooks on the wall. The smell of kerosene and wood ashes in the fireplace still permeated the room—the sweet, musky odor that always lingered long after the fire had died.

I recognized the old piece of floral linoleum that had served as a rug. The one window in the room had an Irish lace curtain over it, but it was yellow now instead of the starched white I remembered. Over the fireplace still hung a sepia photograph of Zerelda's father. He was sitting up very straight, wearing a dark suit and white shirt. No tie, but his shirt was buttoned all the way up to the neck as if he was formally dressed.

I didn't remember ever examining the photograph closely, so I walked over and looked at it carefully. It was hard to tell if Zerelda's father was a black man or a white one. His eyes must have been blue or green, because they weren't dark in the photograph. His nose was very straight, almost European, and he had angular cheekbones. His dark hair, however, was curly and styled in oily waves. The photograph was centered in an oval wooden frame with no mat board. The glass in the frame was wrinkled with age—it seemed to be thicker at the bottom than at the top.

When I finished examining the picture, I walked over and sat down in the rocking chair. It was as if I was a child again, with Zerelda and Jim ready to come walking in at any moment.

The bedroom was behind the sitting room, the door closed. I walked over, opened it and went inside. An old iron headboard and footboard leaned against the wall. I remembered the bed from the day Zerelda died. I still remember it. There was nothing else in the room. It was dark because there were shutters over the windows, and they were closed. I walked over to the nearest window and opened the shutters.

***

I found myself staring right into Luther Summerfield's blood-shot eyes a few inches away. His nose was pressed against the window and I could smell the whiskey on him through the cracks in the glass. A huge jolt of fear went through my entire body. In a panic I reached for the cell phone in my pocket but it fell out onto the floor.

My mind was racing. What should I do? I couldn't lock the door..it had no locks. I couldn't run away: there was only one exit from the room, and that led straight to Luther. I bent down and scrabbled on the floor for the phone. When I looked back up at the window, Luther was gone.

I didn't know where he was. In a frenzy I shut the door and pulled the iron footboard from along the wall and forced it up under the doorknob.

Feeling a little more secure, I began dialing frantically. First Hank, then Greg. Both numbers were busy.

"Jesus. Jesus," I said to myself. "Jesus, help me." Tears were streaming down my face. My heart was beating so hard I thought I might be having a heart attack. I leaned against the wall to catch my breath and try to slow down the rhythm of my heart. I kept speed-dialing Greg, but his line continued to be busy. Hank was in Charleston—too far away to help—so I knew it was no use to continue calling him. I tried Greg's number one more time. Busy.

Suddenly there were footsteps in the house. Heavy footsteps. "Oh, God. Oh, Jesus," I said as I dialed the phone again, "Please let Greg answer this time." The line was still busy, and the footsteps were getting closer. Then just as they stopped outside the door to the bedroom, there was a loud explosion. Then another.

I heard the sound of someone running across the floor and a door slamming. Then, of all things, I heard Adelle say in a low angry voice, "Get 'yo white ass away from that door, Mr. Summerfield, or I'm go blow 'yo head clean off."

I dialed again. This time it rang through.

"Sheriff's office…"

"Get Greg on the phone."

"I'm sorry, the sheriff is on another line, can I take a message?"

"Hell, no. I need to speak to him and I need to speak to him right now." I was yelling into the phone.

There was silence on the other end of the line and then Greg answered.

"Greg, Greg, help me." I was hysterical.

"Who is this?"

"Greg, it's Emily. Please. Help me. I'm in the old cabin at the house. Help me."

"Emily?"

"Greg, help me."

"Slow down, Emily. I'm on the way. What's the matter?"

"Luther Summerfield. He's drunk. He's here. I just heard two loud gunshots. Adelle's here too. Adelle must have shot him. I'm in the old bedroom and…" The phone cut off. The battery was dead.

The silence was terrifying. It seemed to go on forever. Then I heard Adelle's voice: "Come on out, Miss Emily," she called through the door. "Luther ain't 'gonna hurt you. I got him covered."

I wasn't so sure she was right, but I moved the footboard away from the door and cracked it open. I could see Luther backed up against the fireplace and Adelle glaring at him. She had her hand in her sweater pocket and seemed to be hiding the gun she had fired, pointing it at him. There was a walking stick in her other hand. The smell of liquor in the room was overwhelming.

"Okay, Luther," Adelle said. "Sit down in that chair."

Luther moved over to the side of the room. He staggered against the wall a couple of times and then grabbed the back of the chair to keep his balance. When he was in the chair, Adelle said, "Miss Emily, take off your belt and tie his hands up behind him."

I tied him up, trying not to gag from the smell of whiskey and Luther's body odors. He had been sick; dried vomit was all over the front of his shirt.

Adelle poked at him with her stick and said, "'Fess up. What you doin' here?"

Luther's head was hanging down. He had a bad color— almost green. I was afraid he was going to start vomiting again, but he didn't.

Adelle jabbed at him harder with her walking stick. "Fess up, fool, 'cause you in a heapa trouble." She turned to me and said, "Miss Emily, you better call up the High Sheriff and tell him we needs him down here. We done caught ourselves a rat."

"I already talked with him, Adelle. He's on his way."

Adelle jabbed at Luther again, "I told you to 'fess up."

I said, "Leave him alone, Adelle, he's too drunk to help us."

Adelle and I sat down on the sofa to wait for Greg. Suddenly, Luther began to cry.

My daddy always said there was nothing worse than a maudlin drunk. He was right. Luther started talking and crying at the same time. "I didn't mean any harm," he said, "I was just looking for information. Looking for information."

"Luther," I said, "Look at me."

His head stayed down. He was sobbing, and snot was running out of his nose.

"Luther, we know what your father told you. We know you have a brother. Max told us."

"Yeah," Adelle said, "We know 'bout that and we know other stuff too."

"You don't know," Luther said. "You don't know. She's dying. My grandbaby's dying. That nigger wouldn't tell me. She wouldn't tell me where he was."

"Where who was?" I wanted to slap his face. He was talking about Marie. He had described Marie as a nigger, just as I had years earlier, before my daddy set me straight. It made me furious. I gritted my teeth together and clenched my jaw, "Where who was, Luther? Who were you looking for?"

"Charlie. That kid of hers." He squirmed in the chair and I noticed he had wet his pants. "She said it was none of my business about her baby or anybody else's baby. She was telling me to leave. Telling me I could rot in hell. Then she just fell over. Fell on the floor. I told her 'Don't you die on me, you old black bitch. Don't you die on me.' But she wouldn't move. She wouldn't move off the floor. Wouldn't move."

Luther glanced up at me and a mean look came over his face. "All I could find were a few old letters. They didn't tell me anything. She had written them. They didn't tell me anything. Nothing."

Luther began sobbing loudly again. "There was nothing there. Nothing. I couldn't find nothing."

At this moment Greg and two deputies walked in the door, and Luther quit talking.

"Oh, Greg, thank God you're here."

"Mr. Greg. This man's a drinking fool and don't have no business being 'round here. He just about scared Miss Emily slap to death," said Adelle.

I cut in, "He was there when Marie died, Greg. He was there."

"Stop. Stop it. Y'all are talking all over each other," Greg said. He shook his head and turned to Adelle. "Tell me what happened, Adelle."

"Well, I got to thinking 'bout Miss Emily walking over here all by herself. It's been a long time since she's been in this cabin. I decided to walk over and check on things myself. Just as I got here, I noticed a big rat hangin' round." She pointed her walking stick at Luther. "He didn't see me, he was holdin' on to the walls of the house, trying to steady his self. I saw him go in the house." She walked over in front of Luther and stared at him. "He was slobbering drunk and threatening like. Uh-huh, I had to do something."

Greg looked at me. "What happened next, Emily?"

"That's when I heard the gunshots and Adelle saying it was okay for me to come out of the room. We tied Luther in the chair after that."

Greg shook his head and told the deputies to untie Luther. "Luther, you must like that jail cell downtown," he said, "because that's where you're heading."

The deputies removed the belt that was holding Luther to the chair, and gave it to Greg. When they pulled Luther to his feet, he was still staggering drunk, but he looked as if he was beginning to sober up. I knew he was going to have a hell of a hangover.

Greg held my belt out to me. "You want this, don't you?"

"No. I don't want it. I'll enjoy getting rid of it though." I swung the belt back and forth a couple of times then threw my arms around Greg's neck. "Thank God you're here, Greg. Thank God."

Greg pulled back. I guessed that with his deputies there he was conscious of his dignity and position, so I took my arms from around his neck and backed away.

Greg said, "I don't think he would have hurt you, Emily. He was drunk."

"I know. I know that now, but I was really scared when I first saw him through the window."

Adelle was shuffling around the room. She had taken out a small bottle from an orange potion bag and was sprinkling its contents in the corners of the room. It smelled like ginger, powerful enough to overcome all the other smells in the cabin. I remembered Adelle used African ginger when working with spirits, but I wanted her confirmation of it.

"Adelle, what are you doing?"

"I'm putting out a potion to keep out the evil spirits...and rats." She turned around and gave Luther an ugly look.

Greg said, "Adelle, you need to give me your gun. It isn't registered, is it?"

"No, sir."

"Well, let's have it."

"Ain't got no gun." Adelle patted her pocket. "Don't need no gun when I gots cherry bombs." She pulled out two more from her pocket.

Greg started laughing. "Damndest thing I've ever seen in law enforcement. You've captured a man using cherry bombs."

After they hauled Luther away, Adelle and I sat down in the living room of the cabin.

"Adelle, I want the truth. Do you know why Marie spent so much time in this cabin before she died?"

"She was memorin'. She was memorin' 'bout those gone by days and the baby. Zerelda's baby." She leaned up in her rocking chair and pulled out her pipe.

"Tell me, Adelle, what did she say happened?"

"She say that after you and Mr. Hank came runnin' up to the house, she hot-footed it over here to the cabin. Found Zerelda all hole up in the bed, just like y'all said, and a baby already born. She picked up the baby and ran him outside."

"Ran him outside? Why'd she do that?"

"'Cause there weren't any running water in the house, that's why. All they had was that old hand pump in the yard and it was half broke. She came outside to the washing tub to rench off the baby and clean him up."

"It was a boy?"

"Yes ma'am. Marie said it was a boy and he was plenty mad about being pushed out into the world before his time."

"What do you mean before his time?"

"He was early. Marie said he wasn't much bigger than her hand. Teensy little thing."

"Well, why did everybody lie and say the baby died?" The new information was tearing up my mind. Hank and I had talked recently about the graves in the cemetery. Jim's grave and Zerelda's grave with the baby; she and the baby were buried together. The tombstone said so. Marie and my daddy had told me about the baby in the casket...told me the little thing was dressed in a blue baby gown and placed in Zerelda's arms. They saw the undertaker close the casket.

Adelle hadn't answered. "Why did everybody lie and say the baby died?"

"Ain't nobody lied. Nobody ain't lied about nothing, Miss Emily. Just ain't nobody said nothing, either."

"Well, I call it lying. Saying Jim and Zerelda's baby was dead when it wasn't dead—that was lying. Telling Jim his only child was dead—it was cruel and inhuman."

Adelle had her arms folded, and she was staring me down. "Missy, you don't know what you're talking about." She glanced down and ran her hands over her dress to straighten it over her knees, then looked back up at me. "Guess there's no use to keep the secret any longer."

"What secret, Adelle?"

"There was two babies."

"Two babies?"

"There was two babies."

"How do you know, Adelle?"

"I knows because Marie told me so. She said there was two babies born. One born dead and one born kicking. She say when she went back up in the cabin, Zerelda was dead. She had birthed another baby. It was still tied up to her but it was dead, just like Zerelda. They was both dead and there weren't nothing Marie could do to change it. Marie said she knowed right away there was 'gonna be trouble 'bout the baby."

"Trouble?"

"Yes ma'am. Trouble. The dead baby in the bed with Zerelda was a black baby. Marie said the one she was totin' was a white baby."

"You're not serious...a black baby and a white baby? Twins?"

"They weren't look-alikes. Two sacks. There was two sacks. And the black baby—he wasn't very black at all, but Zerelda—she wasn't very black, neither. And the white baby? She said the baby had nappy-looking hair but he had a white face."

I thought of the photograph of Zerelda's father over the fireplace. He looked white—perhaps with a mixed heritage, so the idea of Zerelda having a child with light skin wasn't far-fetched. White people consorting with black people was a well-known fact of life during the days of slavery, and varying degrees of skin color were possible for just about anyone who claimed slaves as ancestors; it was also possible for people who didn't claim their connection to slavery to vary in skin color. Also, I knew when black babies are born they are pink, and their skin darkens within a few hours.

"I still don't understand, Adelle. What happened to the baby? Why didn't Marie tell Jim about the other baby?"

Adelle stomped her foot and said in a loud voice, "That second baby weren't Jim's. It was too white. Jim was too black—blue gum black. People was already saying Jim was too old to get himself a baby." She paused and shook her head. "'Ree said Jim's heart was gonna be all broke up 'bout Zerelda and the dead baby. There weren't no need for him to get all broke up about a baby that weren't none of his—so she took the baby and hid 'em."

"Hid him? Where?"

"She said she wrapped the baby up in a blanket and hid him down in the cellar room to the big house to keep him warm 'til she could take him away."

"Where'd she take him?"

"She said she first took him over to the mid-wife's house to have him checked out and have that silver stuff put in his eyes so he wouldn't go blind. Then she took him away and hid 'em. I don't know where, but I 'spect her sister's got 'em. Marie never said so, but that's what I suspect."

Adelle was right. I knew it in my gut. Zerelda was at least three-quarters white, and if the baby's father was white, then the missing baby could have been too white for Jim to accept as his own. The mixed ancestry of Zerelda's parents could definitely have produced fraternal twins with different skin colors.

I knew the twins were the products of the same father in spite of Adelle's confusion, so I said, "Who was the father of the baby, Adelle?"

"Don't know. I asked Marie 'bout it lots of times, but she wouldn't say anything. She just told me to stick to my own business."

I was still confused. I suspected the twin's father had to be Luther's father. That was the only connection to the money orders and the checks. Marie must have been blackmailing him. But even with this new information, one thing still troubled me: why had Mr. Summerfield mentioned Marie in his will, after he had been so secretive through the years? How could Marie, a woman I loved and trusted, be a blackmailer? And where was Charlie?

"Adelle, why didn't you tell anybody about this before?"

"'Cause Marie swore me off it. She told me right after the baby was born. She never mention it again. When I'd bring it up she'd swell like a pouting pigeon and walk away. I didn't know nothing 'bout Mr. Summerfield 'til today when I was in the laundry room and heard y'all talking. Figured it out."

Indeed. Marie had known the truth all along. She'd had a dark side to her character that allowed her to lie to an old man about a baby, hide the baby away and blackmail another man I suspected was the baby's father. I decided I had never really known Marie.

Adelle and I walked back to the house. We were a pair of cripples—the walking wounded. She was shuffling along, slowed by her old age and the gout in her foot; I was shuffling along on my gimpy knee because I didn't have my crutches to lean on. My leg was throbbing with every step.

Adelle had her walking stick and we hadn't gone far when she noticed me limping. "You can't get far on that leg, Missy. You needs help. I needs to cut you a walking stick too. Sit down. I'll help you back up when it's time."

I sat down on the grass and she leaned against a pecan tree while she stripped the branches off a small limb. I looked back toward the old cabin and began to cry. The day's events had unsettled me and I needed a dose of estrogen; I had left my pills in Savannah.

"Adelle, there was nothing in that old cabin. Just nothing at all. I don't remember it being that way. Jim and Zerelda lived in horrible poverty. No running water. No heat. No appliances. Horrible poverty. I've thought about the cabin over the years but I've never thought of how bare it was. I remember it as being a warm and wonderful place to be. I didn't recognize how terribly poor they were, how little they must have had."

Adelle looked over at me and said, "You were just blinded to it. The love blinded you to it...shielded you away from the sadness."

"But no one ever discussed the poverty, Adelle. It was never mentioned. That's what bothers me. It was never... ever...mentioned."

"Lots of things weren't mentioned, chile. There was lots of

things white folks didn't take seriously 'bout the way we used to live. Some of 'em are still blinded to it." She paused and took her pipe out of a pocket, but didn't light it. "To recognize things, folks would have to trade shoes, try it out, get to know each other's opinions in life together..."—Adelle was as serious as I had ever seen her—"...and that ain't going to happen."

"What do you mean it's not going to happen?"

"Both races was shielded from each other in those days, Miss Emily. What we were taught, that's all we went by and that's all you went by. What people told us until we were a certain age is all we could know until we learned something else on our own. Back then, people was taught the way their ancestors taught them. Everybody weren't taught together. We was segregated in our thinking too. White folks thought black folks was crazy and black folks thought white folks was crazy when we was segregated, 'cept white folks didn't get their feelings hurt as much. They thought they was more dignified."

I thought about the different entrances and water fountains I had seen as a child: one designated for whites, the other for coloreds.

"Jesus, Adelle. That was a crazy system, wasn't it?"

"It was crazy. We was segregated away from each other, and then the next thing you know, we was fighting a war together. Ain't that something? We was fightin' a war together. Guess color don't matter when you in the ditch and dying."

She finished stripping the branches off the limb and handed it to me. I wasn't ready to leave.

"Adelle, why did Marie spend so much time in the old cabin during the weeks before her death?"

"She was taking away stuff to put in her trunk. Important stuff. Stuff she said Zerelda had hidden away in the fireplace bricks under the mantle. She'd been lookin' for them a long time. 'Least that's what she told me."

"But there weren't any letters or papers in the trunk at Marie's house, Adelle. There were no papers at all, anywhere in the cabin, except for the few scattered in the room. The trunk was just stuffed full of..."

"No ma'am. Not that trunk. That one's the doll trunk where Marie kept her baby doll clothes. I'm talking about the other trunk. The one hidden in the wall by the fireplace."

"There's another trunk?" The events of the day were beginning to make me wonder if a conspiracy was afoot. Two babies. Two trunks. I wondered if other 'twos' of information were lurking about—waiting to be discovered.

"We've got to go over there and get the trunk, Adelle."

"How come? Ain't nothing in it but some old papers and letters. That's what Marie said."

"How do you know? You haven't read the letters, have you?"

"No. I ain't read the letters. I coulda', though."

"Then let's go over there. Let's go over there now."

We argued about it all of the way back to the house. It wasn't a long hike, but even with the help of the walking stick my knee was throbbing and beginning to swell.

Adelle said her head hurt too. "I needs to rest up 'fore I goes anywhere," she said.

It took a great deal more persuasion before Adelle finally agreed to go with me. After we took a couple of aspirin apiece, we climbed into her old Plymouth and headed to Marie's house.

***

It took us about twenty minutes to get there. Even though

it was late in the afternoon, there was still good light. Adelle drove her car right up to the steps and got out.

"Adelle, do you need to check around before we go in?"

She didn't answer. She got out of the car and walked up the steps to the house. Turning around she said, "Nobody's been here. The clean sweep's still here. Ain't nobody been here."

She was right. Someone had cleaned up the yard and a clean swept yard meant you could always tell if something or someone had been lurking about. A clean swept yard was especially useful during snake-crawling season. The trail of a slithering snake could be seen quickly and clearly in a clean swept yard. So could the footprints of an intruder.

I had the key to the house, and I unlocked the door. When I reached inside for the switch and turned the lights on, I was relieved and grateful they were working.

"Wait just a minute," Adelle said as she walked past me into the room. She reached up and felt above the door frame. "Yep, it's still working. I knew it was here."

"What are you talking about, Adelle?"

"The Coon Root. I put it over the door last time we was here, to keep peoples out. They ain't been here, neither, has they?" She grinned, dusted her hands and said, "Lock that door."

I locked the door behind us.

Adelle sat down on a chair. "I can't go no further. I'm wore out."

"Okay, Adelle. You sit there. Now tell me where the other trunk is hidden."

"Right over there in the wood box next to the fireplace. Open the door. You'll see it."

Lots of old houses in the South had wood boxes. Some

were built into the chimney, others just sat out in the room. Marie's wood box was built in and had a door like a cupboard. I pulled the pin from the latch and opened it. All I could see were logs stacked up on top of each other.

"Adelle, there's nothing here but logs."

"Move the logs. You'll see it. You'll see the trunk sittin' right back in there."

I moved the top log, then another…and another. A giant cockroach scurried out.

"Look out for that Yankee butterfly," Adelle said and chuckled. We sometimes called roaches by that name. Others chose to call them Palmetto bugs or water bugs. To me, they were just nasty cockroaches.

I had removed half the logs when I saw the trunk. It was jammed into the back of the wood box. I had to finish removing the remaining logs before I could get it out. Pieces of bark, dirt and another roach—dead this time—came out with the trunk as I pulled it forward.

"We gonna' have to clean up the mess when we leave," Adelle said.

I didn't answer: I was too anxious to get into the trunk. It wasn't large, but it wasn't small, either—about the size of a small washtub. It had the traditional clasp, with a lock in the front and the lid hinged on the back. I tried to open it, but it was locked.

"It's locked, Adelle. I'm going to have to break it open. I'm going into the kitchen for a knife."

"Don't do that."

"Don't get a knife?"

"No. Don't bust it open, neither. Marie said there was a key in the wood box."

I looked inside and didn't see anything. "There's no key here, Adelle."

"Yes there is. Marie told me so. Let your eyes get adjusted. You'll see it."

I waited and, sure enough, there in the very back of the wood box was a small key hanging on a tack. I removed it and opened the trunk.

An autographed photograph of Diana Ross rested on top; I guessed Charlie must have sent it to her. Beneath the picture were neatly folded layers of baby clothes. I removed them carefully and found large manila envelopes. The flaps weren't stuck down, just fastened with the metal tabs. Inside were packets of old letters. The scent of moth balls and the odor of decay made my eyes water, and I began to sneeze.

There were three packets. Each of them was tied with a ribbon, and the letters inside seemed to be arranged in sequence by date. While most were written in ink, a few of them were in pencil. I removed the ribbon and opened the first packet. It was full of letters from Marie to Charlie. There were no envelopes. The letters were all folded neatly and in sequence, with dates at the top of each. The first one was dated 1948.

The letters in the second packet were from Charlie to Marie. They didn't have envelopes, either, but they were in sequence too. The last one was dated March 1989. I figured he must have sent them back to her for safekeeping or something.

The final batch was different. They were letters addressed to Zerelda at a New York City address, and they were still in their original envelopes with postmarks dating back to the late thirties. I looked over at Adelle; she had fallen asleep in the chair. I opened the first letter and read it.

> *Dear Zerelda,*
> *Your letter arrived today. You can't know how much*

I miss you. Thank you for letting me know where you are. I have been sick with worry since you disappeared. I'm so glad that you are safe and with your family in New York.

My darling, won't you please come back? Won't you please come back to me? I don't know that I can live without having you near me. You can live in Charleston or Savannah. I'll pay for it. We can still be together. No one will have to know. You'll never have to clean house for anyone ever again.

The days are too long without you. I can't sleep at night for thinking about you, Zerelda. I want to hold you in my arms again. I'm a miserable man. Please come home.

I love you,

A. S.

P.S. It would be best if you didn't write to me until I have my own address. Until then, please know how much I need you in my life. Please don't forget me.

The initials had to stand for Arthur Summerfield. I had hated Mr. Summerfield all of my life, but tears were welling up in my eyes. I opened another letter.

Dearest Zerelda,

I learned the truth from my parents today. I know they sent you away after they discovered us together. They are set in their ways and don't understand how much we love each other. They don't know I'm writing to you. They have threatened to disinherit me if I try and contact you, but I am writing just the same. I can't help the fact that I love you.

The marsh is turning green again. When I look at it,

all I can think about are those days we spent together and how your green eyes matched the marsh.

I am not dating anyone. I am waiting for you. Have faith, Zerelda, some day we'll be together again.

I love you,

A.S.

P.S. I have gotten a post office box. You can write me here in Yemassee. The address is on the envelope. I can't wait to hear from you.

I read through several more letters. Mr. Summerfield continued to express a great love for Zerelda in all of them, and as time went by he seemed to grow more anxious. One of his last letters said:

Dearest Zerelda,

Why won't you answer my letters. Don't you know my heart is breaking? I don't know if I can live without you. Please let me hear from you.

I still love you,

A. S.

There were no letters from Zerelda to Mr. Summerfield and, judging from his final letter, she didn't ever write him back.

Dear Zerelda,

I was married earlier today. My new wife is sleeping in the next room and all I can think of is you. I hope you will have a happy life without me. I know I will never be as happy again as I was with you.

A. S.

By the time I got to the final letter, tears were streaming down my face and I was sobbing out loud. Adelle woke up.

"What you sniveling for?" she said.

"I can't help it, Adelle. I've been reading these old letters to Zerelda. I think they were written by Arthur Summerfield. He loved her, Adelle. He really loved her."

"That old goat? What business did he have writing to her? How you know it was him?"

"I don't. I don't know for sure, but the initials A.S. are the same as his, and after what Luther said it just stands to reason A. S. means Arthur Summerfield."

Adelle's eyes had narrowed to little slits and she had a perplexed look on her face. "And they could stand for Amos Simpson or Antoine Smith." Adelle snorted her disapproval and said, "I'm going to the wash room. Be back in a minute. Arthur Summerfield, huh!"

***

While she was in the bathroom, I thumbed through the letters from Charlie to Marie. I couldn't find an address mentioned in any of them. Every one of the letters seemed to say just about the same thing: Charlie was having fun; Charlie was playing in a new band; Charlie missed his momma; Charlie wanted to come home, but was just too busy.

Asshole, I thought. Charlie, you are an asshole. I heard Adelle shuffling back into the room as I began gathering up the letters to put them away.

"Not much to go on here, Adelle. Think I'll pack everything up and move the trunk to the house."

As I leaned over to put the first package of letters back in, I noticed something black sticking out under the bottom panel of the trunk. It looked like human hair. I reached down and tried to pull it out, but I couldn't budge it. It was stuck underneath the panel. I leaned into the trunk and tugged on it with both hands as hard as I could.

Suddenly the bottom panel gave way, and when I pulled it out I saw what was hidden there. It was what was left of a doll, lying face down in the bottom of the trunk. I turned it over. A small orange sack tied with a string, and a couple of chicken feathers, were stuffed in its mouth.

"Look at this, Adelle, look at what I've found," I called as I pulled the wooden doll from its hiding place. The doll's jaw had been broken at some time, and it had been glued back together so crudely that its face had a hideous drooling look. The doll's eyes were in a fixed position, staring straight ahead. It was wearing a red t-shirt emblazoned with Beale Street Blues and Barbecue on the front. Two buttons were pinned on the shirt sleeves. One said Memphis BBQ—So good it'll make your tongue slap your brains out; the other promoted the 1975 New Orleans Jazz Festival. I removed them and looked closely at the button backs to see if I could discover which club had handed them out or where they were purchased; but nothing was there.

The doll was lying face up on my lap, and as I turned it over and looked closer I realized it was what was left of some sort of small marionette. The string at the back of its neck that controlled the mouth was gone and its beaver skin hat was crushed. The strings were also missing on its hands and feet. When I sat the doll up in my lap a couple of the chicken feathers came loose and fell to the floor.

Adelle started screaming the minute she saw those chicken feathers. I had never seen her look so scared. She was no stranger to voodoo warnings and she came from a long line of panicky women, but when she ran out into the yard and got into the car, I knew it was time to quit. I sat the doll carefully back down in the trunk, replaced the letters and locked it. I picked the trunk up—it wasn't heavy—and carried it down to the car.

"Don't you go puttin' that thing in this car," Adelle said. "Somebody's put the root on it."

"Adelle, there's nothing in here that will bother you. I want to take the letters home before something happens to them."

Adelle didn't say anything and sat sullenly in the driver's seat. She was on edge and fidgeting.

"Give me the keys, Adelle. I'll put it in the trunk."

"You ain't got that doll and those chicken feathers in there, does you?"

"Of course not," I lied.

She handed the keys to me. When I walked back around and opened the car door, she said, "Somebody's messin' with us. Somebody is messin' with us in a bad fashion. Bad fashion. We gots to study up. We needs to uncross the chicken feathers. Did you leave 'em in his mouth?"

I looked at her and realized she was not joking. She was really scared. I had never seen Adelle afraid of anything. She suddenly seemed older and more fragile.

"Adelle, don't you think Marie put those chicken feathers in the doll's mouth? Don't you think she did that to scare everybody away?"

"No. If she wanted to scare 'em off and protect somethin', the feathers would've been on top of the trunk along with some High John the Conqueror root. Somebody's messin' with us, for sho."

She paused for a moment and looked into the rear view mirror. Then she continued talking, this time to herself. "First thing I gots to do is fix a trouble sheet and pray on it. I gots to ask the Lord to take the root off the doll."

"Adelle, maybe the chicken feathers don't mean anything. Maybe they were put there with the little orange sack just to scare us."

"Maybe so. Maybe not so...and that's what's got me worried. I don't know what they done put in the sack. That's the worst kind of spell. The kind that gets you all confused. Like we is right now. See? We is confused. We can't figure out nothin'. Someone must've put confusion oil all around us. That's what it is—confusion oil."

She was driving carefully, looking right and left along the road as if someone might be lurking there waiting for us. A deer, startled by the headlights, stopped in the road in front of us and Adelle slammed on brakes, missing the deer by a few feet.

"Oh, Lord, Jesus," Adelle said, "See what I mean? Someone's messin' with us."

"Damn it, Adelle, nobody's messing with us. The deer just ran out in the road and was caught in our headlights. A deer in the road doesn't mean anything."

"That's what you think, Missy. That's what you think." Adelle was really worked up.

"If someone is putting a spell on us, Adelle, why don't you mix up a spell for them?"

"That's what I'm gonna do."

"What are you going to put in it?" I figured I would keep her busy thinking up recipes to keep her mind off the shadows along the road.

"First thing I'm gonna do is find me some Jinx Killer Oil—that'll kill the spell and bring forth some good luck. Next I'm gonna find some Blood Root—no evil will cross blood root. Then I'm gonna get me some Dragon's Blood; I'll mix it up with some hot red pepper—that'll help with the uncrossing."

Talking about the potions didn't seem to alleviate any of Adelle's fear. When we got back to my mother's house, it took a pint of vodka and two barbecue sandwiches to calm her down. After that she was too drunk to drive, so she slept upstairs in Marie's old room. I left a light on for her in case she woke up and thought the haints had her.

I sat in the living room for a long time reviewing the day. I hadn't found any concrete information on Charlie, but at least I now knew he had a connection to Beale Street in Memphis, as well as a link to Diana Ross.

I felt a growing sense of urgency, as if I was running out of time. Find Charlie. Find Charlie...Find Charlie...my inner voice kept saying.

The next morning Adelle was in the laundry room acting like she had just gotten to work. "Mornin', Miss Em, you hungry?"

"I'm hungry, Adelle, what about you?"

"I already ate. Made some hoe cakes and shrimp gravy. Want some?"

"No thanks. How in the hell can you eat hoe cakes and shrimp gravy when you've been drinking the night before?"

"Easy. It greases your insides up and dulls the head ache."

"Why didn't you use your old collard and vinegar remedy? It's supposed to cure a headache in under an hour."

"You know collards ain't no good in hot weather. What's the matter with you?" Her mood softened and she chuckled, "Your momma said my breakfast was disgusting. She eats like a chicken, you know. Little pecks of food. She's already up and gone herself."

"Adelle, do you think my mother is avoiding me? I've been home a couple of weeks and I've only seen her two times. I feel like I'm a child again."

"She ain't avoiding you. That's just her acting natural. I sometimes goes two days without seein' her. Only reason I know she's still living is the little check she gives me, and her dirty clothes. Dead people don't dirty up clothes, and she's got plenty washin' for me to do. She must change 'em three times a day and more so on Sunday. And if it ain't clothes, it's sheets..."

Adelle kept chattering, but I ignored her. I was thinking about Marie's trunk and the doll hidden in the bottom. "Adelle, do you think there may be a reason Marie had the...'thing'... hidden in the trunk?" I didn't want to call it a doll since the very mention of the word made her nervous.

"Now what you think? 'Course she had a reason. She didn't want nobody to find it. It was protecting the letters."

"I know that Adelle, but do you think she was trying to tell us something? That the hidden...'thing'...was some kind of clue? Do you think it was a clue to look for Charlie in Memphis?"

"A clue? What about the sack and the feathers? That's a clue for 'sho. A clue to get up and get out of there...and get out of there fast on your feet."

"Damn it, Adelle, if you think the feathers and the sack are a problem, mix up a damned uncrossing potion and I'll take it back over there myself. I'm not scared." I slammed my fist down on the table. "Cook up some of that stuff you were talking about last night. I'm not asking about the chicken feathers, I'm asking about the damned doll. Could the doll, t-shirt, and buttons be clues...damned clues...to finding Charlie?" I was yelling. "Charlie...I've got to find Charlie."

My hysteria didn't faze Adelle. "Don't ask me. If'n you wants to know about Charlie, you gots to ask Annie. She can tell you all about him, if she has a mind to. I don't know nothing about where that man is. Nothing." Adelle walked back into the laundry room and shut the door.

The coffee pot was still almost full, but the coffee was cold. I poured a cup and put it in the microwave. I was hungry too, so I grabbed an apple and the morning paper and sat down at the table.

***

The screen door slammed just as the microwave buzzed. It was Max.

"Well, well, well...if it isn't Sleeping Beauty. 'Bout time you got up. Adelle tells me that y'all had a good scare yesterday."

"Oh, Max, you can't imagine."

"Yes I can. I've seen Luther Summerfield drunk before. I can't believe he was dumb enough to come over to the cabin, though, drunk or not."

"Well, he was. And I was scared. I don't remember ever being that scared. He's back in jail."

"No, he's just supposed to be. I saw him a little while ago. He was back at the hardware store."

"You're kidding. He's already out of jail?" Max poured himself a cup of cold coffee and sat down across from me.

"Yep. He was hungover as all get out, though. Sort of sad, too." Max looked over at me and saw the fear in my eyes. "Jeez, I'm not trying to upset you. Thought you'd like to know where he was, that's all."

"My God, Max. What if he starts following me again?"

"Luther's not going to do that. Least I don't think he is. If it's worrying you, get a restraining order. Put that lawyer brother of yours to work. Or you can get a handgun. Blow his brains out next time he scares you."

"Max I don't believe in guns."

"Then call your brother." Max stood up and put his cup in the sink. He headed toward the door, then thought better of it and sat back down at the table.

"One more thing, Emily."

"What's that?"

"Luther had a terrible hangover but he asked me what you were doing at the cabin. He's still fixated on finding a brother. He was using the "n" word in every other breath and..."

"God, I hate him. He's the first person I ever heard use the "n" word. I hate people who use that word."

"Don't be so sanctimonious, Emily. You've used it yourself."

Max was agitated. His observation went straight to its mark: I was just as guilty as Luther on occasion. "Yes, Max. I've used that hateful word a couple of times and I'm not proud of it. Who hasn't?"

"Everybody has—if they tell the truth. Luther just uses it because he's too dumb to know better. He's a bigot and you're not. Now what were you doing at the cabin?"

"Hank said Marie spent a lot of time over there before she died. I was just curious, that's all."

"Did you satisfy your curiosity?"

I wasn't ready to share the story about Zerelda's babies, so I gave him half of the truth.

"Not really. Adelle finally told me Marie had two trunks, so we went over to Marie's house and looked through it."

"Two trunks? You found another one?"

"Yep. Marie had it hidden in her wood box. Luther never would have found it there."

"What was in it?"

"Lots of old letters—to and from Charlie—and an old marionette-type doll. That's all."

"She had a doll in the trunk?" Max pulled his hat back on his head and scratched his forehead. "I wouldn't have thought Marie would hide a doll. Imagine that...she had a doll in the trunk."

"Yes, and its head was all cracked open and it had a mouth full of chicken feathers."

Max laughed out loud, leaned back in his chair and almost lost his balance. He caught the edge of the table with his hand and steadied himself.

"Jesus, Max, chicken feathers are funny, but they're not that funny. I've been humoring Adelle about them for hours."

"I wasn't laughing at the chicken feathers. I was just thinking about your faces when you first saw them. Bet it scared you, didn't it?"

"No. That didn't scare me..."

The door opened. "Tell the truth," Adelle said as she walked in the room. "Tell the truth, Miss Emily. We was both scared last night."

I knew Adelle's dignity was now involved so I said, "Yes, we were both scared."

"Hell, you don't know," Max said, "Marie might have been using those feathers on a boyfriend."

"What you mean?" Adelle said. He had her full attention. She walked over closer to the table and glared at him.

"I'm just joking, Adelle. Those chicken feathers reminded me of an old joke I heard once—a joke about the difference between regular sex and kinky sex."

Adelle turned around and went back into the laundry room saying, "White folks is crazy."

"Okay, what's the joke?" I said to Max.

"Well, if you're into normal sex, you stroke each other with a chicken feather; if you're into kinky sex, you use the whole chicken."

Max laughed even louder than before. He adjusted the cap on his head and said, "Well, I'm headin' back out. Call your brother, Emily. Call him if you're worried about Luther." He stood up and left the room.

Adelle stuck her head out from behind the door. She must have been listening to Max's joke. "You didn't tell him 'bout Zerelda's baby, did you?" Adelle looked worried.

"No. I didn't. Why?"

"'Cause he might slip up and tell somebody, that's why. When you go call Annie?"

"I'm going to call her in a few minutes, Adelle,"

"Well, go ahead and do it now, 'fore something else happens to mess us up."

I walked over to the telephone and opened the drawer underneath the cabinet where my mother kept her address book. I knew I'd find Annie's number there.

She answered the phone on the second ring. I didn't recognize her voice and said, "May I please speak to Annie."

"Speaking."

"Annie, this is Emily Chandler from Yemassee."

There was a long pause on the other end of the phone and then she said, "I've been expecting your call."

"You have?"

"Yes. Marie said you'd be calling me sooner or later."

"She did?"

"Yes, ma'am, she sure did."

"I need to talk to you about Marie and her son Charlie. And there's something else too. Will it be all right if I come visit you tomorrow?"

"'Course it will."

"Will Jesse be there?"

"No. He's working days at the hospital all week."

"Too bad. I'd really like to see him. Oh well, I'll come around noon, okay?"

"Yes, ma'am. Noon time will be okay."

I hung up the phone and called Greg. "Greg, I'd like to take you up on that offer to drive me to Augusta. My knee is a lot better, but my car is in Savannah. I don't think Adelle's old car will make the trip, and I don't want to ask anybody around here for theirs."

"When do you want to go?"

"Early in the morning."

"Tomorrow morning?"

"Yes. I'm in a hurry to talk with Annie."

"I'll see what I can do, Emily, but tomorrow is the busiest day of the week for me. Can I let you know later? I'll drop by when I leave the office, if it's okay."

"Sure," I said, and we ended the conversation.

Greg came by just as the sun was setting. I fixed us a drink and invited him to sit out on the porch with me.

"You look great this evening, Emily. I almost didn't recognize you without that cast on your leg."

"Gee, thanks. I knew you were a breast and butt man, but this is getting ridiculous."

Greg laughed and I did too, because I felt I'd hurt his feelings the last couple of times we'd been together. I hoped the laughter would soften the tension between us.

"Greg, did you ever think we'd be sitting out on this porch again at our age?"

"Nope. In fact, I thought you'd never speak to me again, Emily."

"I wouldn't have, except you got a divorce and waltzed back into my life. Oops—I should have said walked into my life at a funeral."

"You know I've never stopped thinking about you, Emily."

"I know."

"I don't think you do know. Even when I made love to my wife, I was thinking about you...wondering what you were doing...who you were with."

I didn't know what to say. I had always adored Greg, but I didn't remember thinking about him while I was making out with someone else. Afterwards perhaps, but never during.

I knew enough about men to keep my mouth shut. "Greg, let's change the subject. I need to tell you what I've learned from Adelle."

I told Greg everything. About Zerelda and the two babies. About the two trunks. About the love letters from Arthur Summerfield to Zerelda. About the doll in the bottom of the trunk. I told him everything I could remember.

Greg sat quietly and listened until I was through talking. "Do you think Adelle knows more than she's telling you?" Greg said.

"I'm not sure, Greg. I do suspect she knows a lot more than she's telling anyway. The chicken feathers probably have something to do with her loss of memory."

"Chicken feathers?"

I had told Greg about the doll, but I hadn't mentioned the chicken feathers or the clothing on the doll.

"When I opened the trunk and found the doll hidden in the bottom, there were chicken feathers and a small sack stuffed in its mouth. Do you know what that means in voodoo terms?"

"I have no idea. That's one black magic practice I haven't heard of before. Depends on what was in the sack working with the chicken feathers, I suppose." He finished his drink and leaned back in the chair. "Were there pins stuck in the doll?"

"No pins were stuck in it anywhere. It really didn't look like a voodoo doll. It was somehow more bizarre."

Greg shrugged his shoulders and said, "Marie probably put the chicken feathers there to scare people off. That'd be my guess."

"Mine, too. Adelle seemed to think they were a warning of some kind."

"Exactly. A warning to scare away people like you and Adelle." Greg laughed and said, "Tell me more about the doll? Wonder why would Marie hide it away?"

"Don't know. The marionette's head was cracked open...it had been broken before and somebody botched a glue job. The t-shirt it was wearing was clean but the doll sure was old and ragged." I threw my hands up in mock surrender. "The t-shirt had a Memphis blues and barbecue slogan on it; the buttons pinned on it were jazz and blues-oriented too."

"Well those are solid hints as to where he's been playing, Emily. Charlie's a blues musician, isn't he? He could have played with a band in Memphis at some point in his career. Did you find out anything else about him?"

"Not one thing. Lots of letters, but no addresses." A whippoorwill called out to its mate in the distance. We quit talking and listened to the sounds of the Lowcountry night. Lightening bugs were sparkling over the lawn and the crickets were singing. We heard the threatening roar of a bull alligator somewhere way off in the marsh.

Greg rattled the ice in his glass. "Sounds to me like you're finally gaining some ground in your search."

I nodded my agreement. "That's why I want to go and visit Annie. She should have some answers for me."

"Oh, that reminds me," Greg said and he stood up and stretched, "I can't go with you tomorrow but I'll lend you my personal car since you don't think Adelle's car will make it. It has an automatic transmission so it shouldn't give your bum knee any trouble."

I was disappointed, but grateful for the use of his car. "Thanks, Greg. I was looking forward to riding up with you. I'm sorry you can't come."

"Me, too. Are you going to take someone along with you?"

"I'll take Adelle. She'll enjoy the ride. Besides—she hasn't been herself since we found those chicken feathers. All she can talk about is looking for certain roots and oils, and fixing up potions."

Greg grunted and sat back down. He took a last sip from the glass and put it on the table.

"You want another drink?"

"No thanks, Emily. One's enough. Guess I'd better head on home."

"Oops, forgot. Can't have the sheriff drinking and driving. That'd really start tongues wagging."

"One's enough for you too. You need to ride with me to get my car. I've got a long day tomorrow, so let's head out."

**

Greg's car was parked in his garage. It was a Buick—the type of car you'd expect a responsible person to drive.

"This car have any quirks, Greg?"

"Shouldn't have any. I had it serviced last week and the tires checked today."

"That's just like you, Greg. Loving and helpful one minute and running off and getting married to someone else the next."

As soon as I said it, I knew it was a mistake. I could have cut my own tongue out, and I knew I had really hurt him. He clenched his jaw and didn't say anything for a few seconds.

"Have a nice trip, Emily." He leaned over and opened the door for me to get in.

"I'm sorry, Greg. That was uncalled for. I don't know what made me say it."

He didn't answer. He just walked away and didn't turn around to say 'goodbye'. I sat in the car not knowing whether to get out and follow him and apologize again or deal with it later. It was already dark and I still had to go by Adelle's house, so I backed out of the driveway and drove off.

"I'll make it up to you tomorrow, Greg" I said out loud to myself. I was still mad at him—and at the same time I knew I still loved him.

***

There was a light on in Adelle's house when I got there, so I knew she was awake. I honked the horn, rolled down the window and called out her name. She leaned out of the front window to see who was calling.

"Who's there?"

"It's me. Emily. I need to talk with you."

She was suspicious of the car at first but came out on her porch after turning its light on. She was in a dither, looking around as if she expected someone else to be there lurking in the bushes. She was wearing her sailor cap, a fire-engine-red nightgown, and dark brown leather men's slippers on her feet. She had her walking stick in her right hand and was holding it like a weapon. When she reached the car I noticed a peculiar odor. It wasn't perfume. "What's that smell, Adelle?"

"None of yo' business."

"Okay. Maybe it's none of my business, but what is it? It's sweet, but acrid at the same time." Actually, it stunk but I didn't want to hurt her feelings.

Adelle looked around and then leaned in the window. "It's my sellin' potion. I've been mixin' it up tonight. Several folks been askin' for it and I needs some myself. Don't want sales to slack off. Now, missy, what you doin' in that car? How'm I 'spose to know who you is?"

"I borrowed it, Adelle. I borrowed it because I'm going to see Annie in the morning. Do you want to go with me?"

Adelle shuffled her feet and looked around her yard. "You didn't see any deer on your way over here, did you?"

"No. No deer. I haven't seen any animals, and no people either."

"Okay then, I'll go with you. What time we leaving?"

"Early. Do you want me to pick you up?"

"No, ma'am. I gots to do laundry first. I'll get over to the house about first light and get my work done. Then we can go. Don't want to make nobody mad. Friday's payday."

"Okay, Adelle. I'll see you in the morning."

Adelle went back into her house and I headed home.

The next day Adelle had already finished several loads of clothes when I came downstairs. I could smell fresh biscuits and coffee.

"You hungry?"

"No. I'm really not hungry this morning, Adelle. Are you?"

"Yes'm. I've already eaten. Mixed up some biscuits. Want one? You needs to put some food in your stomach or you might get dizzy in the car. Here—let me fix you one." She put a biscuit on a plate and sat it in front of me. "Want some jam?"

"No, thanks. I'll take some coffee, though."

When I looked at the plate, I saw a buckeye sitting on it.

"What's the buckeye for, Adelle?"

"Luck. Put it in your pocket. You needs it."

"Where'd you find it?"

"Don't you go worrying 'bout where I finds things. Just put it in your pocket. That's all you needs for the trip."

I finished my biscuit and coffee and we cleaned up the kitchen.

It took us about two hours to get to Augusta. I drove half way until my knee started throbbing, then Adelle took over.

Annie's house wasn't hard to find. She was waiting for us at the door.

"Y'all come in and take a seat."

We both sat on the antique sofa against the wall under a window. A plate full of sugar cookies was on the coffee table next to a pitcher of lemonade and several glasses.

"Help yourself," Annie said.

"Thank you, but not right now," I said, "I'll wait a few minutes and have some."

Adelle reached into her pocket for her pipe. "Mind if I smoke a little pipe?"

"No smoking in here," Annie said. "Jesse says it'll kill you."

Adelle put the pipe in her mouth anyway but didn't light it. I could tell from the scowl on her face she was ready to leave.

"Go on out on the porch and smoke, Adelle," I said.

Adelle didn't answer. She turned around and walked out onto the porch, shutting the door behind her.

"Annie, you said you were expecting to hear from me. Why?"

"Marie said you'd be calling me, sooner or later." She got up out of her chair and walked over to a closet. She opened its door, pulled out a red velvet box, and handed it to me.

"This is for you. Marie said to give it to you if you ever asked about Charlie. She said to give it to you after she was dead. Only if she was dead. She brought it up here to me not long before she passed."

I looked at the box. The velvet was old and worn around the edges.

"Go ahead. Open it. Marie wanted you to have it."

I opened the box. The contents were covered with tissue paper. I removed the tissue, wondering what I would find underneath.

It was another doll. This one was intact, and it didn't have any small sacks or chicken feathers in its mouth. But there was a difference: this one was a black Charlie McCarthy doll. This dummy's head tilted and could turn all the way around, and it had lifelike moving glass eyes. Its head, hands, torso and feet were made of polyester resin instead of wood, and it had human hair. It was elegantly dressed in a black tuxedo, white shirt front with wing collar, white tie and white shoes. Its top hat was made of simulated fur.

"Annie, what in the world. Why..."

Annie leaned back as if all the air had been let out of her—deflated and tired. When she spoke again her voice was very quiet, almost a whisper. "That's Charlie—Marie's Charlie, Miss Emily. She wanted you to have him. She loved that doll like it was her own child. It broke my heart when she sent him up here a few weeks ago. I knew she was getting ready to die."

"Do you mean that...this doll is Charlie? That there never was a real Charlie?" My head was whirling.

"No." Annie shook her head, "There wasn't any real Charlie. Only in Marie's mind. Charlie was only real in her head."

"But why didn't you tell us? Why did you let us think there was a real Charlie all those years? What about Jesse? Does he know the truth?"

"No. He believes he has a cousin Charlie, just like you did. I'm going to have to tell him the whole truth now that you know it."

"I don't understand..."

"Marie lost her only child, little Charlie, to a fever just after her husband Amos died. She never got over it. We knew she liked to listen to Mr. Edgar Bergen and Charlie McCarthy on the radio, so one day we found a dummy-like doll and gave it to her. 'Fore we knew it, she was collecting even more dolls...talking to them like they was real people...Charlie's friends. If we said something to her about it, she got real mad and all funny-like, so we just played along with her. Acted like there really was a Charlie." Annie looked down at the floor and smoothed her skirt. She seemed embarrassed.

"My husband—before he died—found the first doll at a flea market." Annie looked up and I could see tears in her eyes. "He loved flea markets and that sort of thing. Picked up all sorts of stuff to give Marie—stuff Charlie might have used or needed." She wiped a tear from her eye. "I sure do miss him. Marie, too. I miss them a lot." Her voice was quivering.

"I know you do, Annie." I was getting teary-eyed too.

"It wasn't hurting anybody—and loving those dolls seemed to give her a reason for living, especially after you children were grown up and gone. She was lonely living out in the country all by herself."

"She didn't have to live by herself, Annie. She could have stayed on with us. She chose to live in the country alone. We didn't make her do that." I was getting upset. I hoped that Marie never believed we didn't want her around us—that we wanted her to live alone.

Annie took a sip of lemonade and said, "I know you didn't make her live alone. I think she was afraid y'all were going to hear her talking to her babies. She was looking for privacy... said she wanted to be close enough yet far enough away to tend to you. We begged her to move up here with us, but she wouldn't leave y'all. She was afraid of what would happen to you if she wasn't there to love you and take care of you. If it weren't for Marie, y'all would have had to raise yourselves."

"But why didn't you tell us? We would have understood. We wouldn't have cared. Why didn't you tell us?"

"Tell you? You was too little and so was your brother. Your momma and daddy would've thought Marie was touched in the head, if they knew the truth. She would've lost her job." Annie shook her head. "Crazy. They would've said she was crazy. Nobody would have hired her if they thought she was writing herself letters and talking to dolls. By the time you were grown, it was too late for her to marry and start another family." Annie voice quivered. I saw that her eyes were still moist so I reached in my bag and gave her a Kleenex. She removed her glasses and wiped her eyes. "She just stayed on in Yemassee by herself in that old house of hers at night, and stayed with your momma in the big house in the daytime. She missed you children once you were gone and she felt all responsible for your momma—said your momma was the most helpless woman she had ever seen."

"But what about the other doll? The marionette I found in the old trunk at her house. What about that one?"

"That was the first Charlie, Miss Emily. He just wore out after so much loving from Marie. She hid him away after she broke him. She couldn't bury him in the yard—it would've been bad luck."

"Bad luck?"

"Yes'm. Marie couldn't bury Charlie or that would've meant he was dead. Wouldn't have been real anymore. We figured she just hid 'em away, that's all. Marie was always secretive. She thought as long as everything was hidden, everything was all right. I expect those dolls reminded her of Jesse and her own Charlie before he died."

Annie poured another glass of lemonade and offered it to me. I took a sip. It was the old-fashioned lemonade I loved, the kind Marie used to make for us when we were children. She poured a glass for Adelle too.

"Where did this dummy come from, Annie?" I touched its face and smoothed its jacket.

"My husband and I knew the old one was worn out; we saw it sitting in her bedroom one day. It was broken and she had glued it back together. We didn't have any idea where to find another make-believe doll like it." Annie paused and leaned back in her chair. "Marie loved Charlie McCarthy so we went to the library and looked up information on Mr. Edgar Bergen. You remember him don't you—or are you too young?"

I smiled at Annie. "I remember seeing Edgar Bergen on television, but he was an old man. I remember Charlie McCarthy too. Now that I think about it, Marie loved to watch him with that dummy. They really made her laugh."

"That's right. She loved Mr. Bergen. The library book led us to a company that made the dolls for ventriloquists. We wrote off and ordered a real one for Marie—we ordered one with a black face too. We left it on her porch so she wouldn't know it was from us. She thought the angels brought him to her. That's what she said...the angels brought him to her. She always said angels brought babies down from heaven and took them away too."

At this point we heard Adelle yell at someone outside. I winced because I wasn't sure if she had brought firecrackers or not, and I didn't want her disturbing the neighborhood. I was still confused about Charlie. I heard what Annie told me—that Charlie was a figment of Marie's imagination—yet I was not convinced of it.

I said, "It's still hard to believe. Charlie was always such a real person to me." I finished the glass of lemonade and set it down on the table. As I did, I remembered the letters.

"But what about the letters, Annie? I have the letters." I snatched my tote bag from the floor, took out the packets of letters, and handed one packet to Annie. "Look at these. These are from Marie to Charlie. And these..." I hurriedly put another packet on the sofa beside me, "these are from Charlie to Marie." I still wasn't convinced Charlie was only a doll. He had been a living presence ever since I could remember.

Annie didn't open the packet. She looked sadly at me and

said, "Miss Emily, I told you...I told you Charlie wasn't real. Marie wrote those letters to herself. I knew it even when she read 'em over the phone to me. She kept herself busy at night imagining what her baby might be doing if he had lived. Look at the handwriting. It's all the same, isn't it?" She handed the letters back to me.

I took one letter from each packet and compared them. "Oh Annie, you're right. I can't believe it. The writing is the same. I didn't notice it before."

Annie was rubbing the arm of her chair with her hand. "Marie didn't mean any harm. Charlie was just a part of her life she needed to keep her from going crazy. He kept her from being lonely like. He kept her company."

I couldn't say anything for a moment. The truth was finally clear to me: there had never been a Charlie who played the piano or went to Boy's Catholic in Savannah or toured with Diana Ross and the Supremes. Marie's Charlie had never been anywhere at all. He had only lived in her head and heart.

Before I could ask another question, Adelle came back into the room. "Did you tell her 'bout Zerelda's letters?"

"What about Zerelda?" Annie said.

I took a long breath and almost whispered, "We found another packet of letters in Marie's old trunk, Annie. They were love letters to Zerelda. We think Arthur Summerfield wrote them. We think he was the father of her baby." Annie's eyes widened and she sat back in her chair. "So you know about Zerelda's baby."

"Yes," I said. "It's Jesse, isn't it? Jesse is Zerelda's son?"

Annie was quiet for a moment. She was twisting her wedding ring around on her finger. "Yes. That's what Marie told me about Jesse. Told me he was born a twin and his momma and brother were dead in the bed. Said he was too white to pass for Jim's own child so she took him and hid him away until she brought him up here for me to raise."

"His father's Arthur Summerfield, isn't he?"

Annie looked out of the window for a long time, then said, "I don't know who Jesse's father is. Marie never told me. Said it would trouble things up if I knew. She knew who he was—said he wanted to support the child and gave her money for him. That's how come Jesse's a doctor today. The money Marie sent up here—that money saved Jesse, saved him from being an outcast to blacks and whites both."

"But how did Jesse get into school? Didn't you need a birth certificate?"

"I had one. Marie brought me one with the baby." She walked over to a small desk in the corner and opened the top drawer. Searching through a few papers, she pulled out an envelope and handed it to me.

"That's his birth certificate. Says I am his mother and my husband, God rest his soul, is his father."

"But that's not true. How did Marie get a birth certificate with your name on it, Annie?"

"She said it was easy. She took him over to the hospital in Savannah and told 'em she was me. They gave the baby a checkup and didn't ask any questions about the daddy; just told her to fill out the paperwork. People weren't particular about black babies in those days. They didn't care who the momma or the poppa was. They were just glad the baby was born and okay."

"We was all glad the baby was born and okay," Adelle said. She had been strangely silent until this moment. "But Marie ain't told us who the daddy was. She never told us who he was. She kept that secret to herself. She didn't want nobody knowing who the baby's daddy was."

"Well, I guess we may never know for sure," I said, "but we do have a good idea of who Jesse's father might be. That'll just have to do for now. At least I've found Marie's Charlie." I reached for my bag and stood up to leave.

"Before you go, Miss Emily. There's one more thing I have to give you."

"There is?"

"Yes. Marie left a letter for you too. She brought it up here with Charlie." Annie walked back over to her desk and unlocked the middle drawer. There was only one letter in the cubbyhole and she handed it to me. I recognized Marie's spidery handwriting right away.

I opened the seal on the letter. It was dated three weeks before she died.

Dear Miss Emily,

If you are reading this letter, I am dead and in the ground. There are things I hid from you and I hope you understand I couldn't do things any other way than the way I did.

The times that passed by us made us all different. You and Mr. Hank were always troubled by that day you found Zerelda dying in the bed and so was I. Zerelda put a terrible strain on us. Sometimes I think that's why you and Mr. Hank are the way you are—so stand offish and afraid of loving and all alone with no babies.

Don't be mad at Zerelda. She loved Jim, but she couldn't help herself, she loved Mr. Arthur Summerfield the most. She loved him all her life until the day she died. She ran away from him once, but he found her again when she came back home with Jim. I warned her about seeing him, but it didn't make any difference. They were determined to spend time together. A rich white man and a poor black woman—they didn't have anything to look forward to but trouble in those days.

She was hoping the baby would be dark and pass it off as Jim's baby, but things didn't work out that way. Jesse was too white to be any kin to Jim, that's why I took him away. Weren't any need in stirring up old stories and there wasn't anybody else to take the baby. I had to give him to my sister Annie. She needed a baby and couldn't get one.

I wanted to keep Jesse and raise him up with my Charlie, but I knew that wasn't any good, either. People would be wondering what I was doing with a child that was almost white. And I was scared the baby would grow up looking like his real daddy and that people would recognize him and call him a black bastard.

I told Mr. Arthur about the baby as soon as I could. I never liked the man, but he cried that day and said he wanted to do the right thing. He said he had to pay me through the back door because he didn't want anybody knowing he had a black child. I sent the money on to Annie every time he gave me any.

Before he died, I talked with Mr. Arthur for a long time about Jesse. I believe he was proud of Jesse in spite of Jesse being a black man. He said Mr. Luther never amounted to much.

If you will look inside Charlie's head, you'll find the secret I've been hiding all these years—Jesse's real birth papers. I took him to the hospital in Augusta before bringing him to Annie. Said I was Zerelda and told them Mr. Arthur Summerfield was the daddy. Augusta was far enough away from Yemassee and I knew the secret would be safe.

Jesse has a right to know about his ancestors. Both of his birth parents are dead now, so it won't make any difference.

Love,

Marie Dixon

P.S. Please take care of my Charlie.

Annie and Adelle were both staring at me, waiting for me to explain the contents of the letter. Rather than tell it in my own words, I read the letter to them.

Afterwards, both of them had tears in their eyes, although Annie seemed to be more relieved than saddened to know the truth about Jesse's father.

Adelle stood up and brushed her dress off with her hand. "Well, you goin' to bust his head open and get the paper?"

"Adelle. I am not going to bust his head open. I'm going to try and get its head off without breaking it." I picked the doll up tenderly. It had a hollow back, with its head mounted on a control stick and lever controls for both eyes. When I sat him on my knee he was suddenly more than a doll. He was Marie's legacy. I reached inside the mouth and felt where the neck joined. There was nothing there. I turned my hand and moved my fingers along the top of the mouth and felt a piece of adhesive tape. I pulled it and there it was—an envelope; it had been carefully taped to the inside of the dummy's head.

"What's that?" Adelle said. "What'd you pick out of his head?" Her eyes were big and round.

"I don't know, Adelle. It's an envelope." I opened it and pulled a folded paper out. It was a birth certificate. Jesse's true birth certificate. It read: *Charles Jesse Summerfield. Born October 10, 1948. Father: Arthur Summerfield, Yemassee, South Carolina. Mother: Zerelda Turner, Yemassee, South Carolina.*

"Here, Annie, this is for you," I said and handed it to her.

"This means that Jesse is crazy Luther's brother, don't it." Adelle said. It wasn't a question; she was making a statement. She stood there, lost in thought for a minute, then sat back down on the sofa and leaned forward facing me, "You better tell Annie 'bout Luther's grandbaby."

Before Annie could ask anything, I said, "Annie, Luther Summerfield's granddaughter is dying with leukemia. I don't know what, if anything, Jesse could do to help, but it'll be his decision to make. You have the birth certificate; I know you'll give it to Jesse when the time is right."

I gave her the love letters too. They were a piece of the past, and they would be important to Jesse. I wanted him to know how much his parents loved each other, and I suspect Marie did too, or she would never have directed me to them— even though it was by such a strange and circuitous route.

Nobody had much to say after that, so Adelle and I headed home. I took Charlie with me.

THE MEDICAL COLLEGE OF GEORGIA, AUGUSTA
One week later.

J esse entered the hospital room. He was making his rounds for the day and this was his last stop before heading home. Luther's grandbaby lay in the bed, pale-faced and very quiet. Her eyes were closed. Death wouldn't wait much longer.

Luther Summerfield was sitting in a chair in the corner. He didn't stand up to greet the oncologist, and barely hid his contempt. He had expected a white doctor, but this one had been assigned to him—an almost-white mulatto, God damn it. Even so, he knew he had to show a minimum of politeness for the sake of his granddaughter.

Jesse nodded to the man in the chair and looked at the child's chart. He was reviewing the data when he noticed the address—Yemassee, South Carolina. He looked at Luther quickly and said, "Are you from Yemassee, Mr.............?"

Luther scowled at him and said, "My name's Summerfield. This is my granddaughter Susan...Susan Summerfield. What d'you want to know for?"

Jesse glanced back down at the chart for a moment and then looked up. "Was Arthur Summerfield your father?" he said.

Luther's eyes flashed and he bared his teeth in a parody of a smile. "What the hell has that got to do with anything?"

There was a charged pause as the two men looked at each other. Finally, Jesse said, "If your father was Arthur Summerfield, and you're Luther Summerfield, we're related. He was my father too."

Luther's eyes narrowed and his face turned purple. In the prolonged silence that followed, they could hear the little girl in the bed breathing—small, shallow breaths.

"You think you're my brother? You?" He picked his hat off the table and slapped it against his knee; a cloud of dust rose up and drifted in the bright sunlight streaming through the lone window in the room. Luther doubled up in a paroxysm of coughing. When he caught his breath again he was shaking with fury. The death of his family, the impending death of his granddaughter, the grief and the rage rose up inside him. "The only brother I got is called Charlie, and nobody can find him. He ain't been seen in Yemassee for fifty years. Shit, the very idea..." He suddenly got up from the chair and took a step towards Jesse, pointing at him with a shaking finger.

Jesse stood his ground. "Charlie doesn't exist. You'll find that out some day. Arthur Summerfield was father to both of us. You can hate me all you want, but I could be the person to save your granddaughter."

"No you ain't. There's plenty of cancer doctors around, white ones too."

"Maybe so. But she's my grand-niece as well as your granddaughter, and I have her same blood type. I could be a donor match. Think about it, Luther."

Jesse looked back down at the chart, took his pen and made notes on it. He looked back up at Luther and said, "We're going to give her some new experimental medication; it'll slow down the leukemia for a few weeks, but she's going to need the bone marrow transplant if she's going to live." He left the room and shut the door quietly behind him.

Luther stood in the middle of the floor, looking at the small girl lying so still in the big white bed. Outside, the trees were bending from a sudden breeze. The sun disappeared behind a cloud and the shadows deepened in the room. A single tear ran down Luther's unshaven cheek.

EPILOGUE

I'm back home in Savannah now. It's been several weeks since I found Charlie and discovered his secret. I haven't told anybody but Hank. He's dating a new blonde and says this one's a 'keeper.' We'll see about that.

Max will be sixty-five in a couple of years and comes into his inheritance. He's not leaving, though; says he'll stay on and help my mother as long as she needs him.

Adelle's always threatening to quit working for the 'cold hominy woman' but she still keeps coming back to work every other day. Last time I was home she fixed me up a potion. Said it would help me sleep. It smells terrible so I haven't used it yet. She's also offered to make a love potion for me and Greg, but I don't think we're going to need one.

Jesse had a new headstone made for Jim, Zerelda and his twin brother; it will last longer than the one there before. He had it inscribed with part of a verse from the hymn "Amazing Grace":

I once was lost but now am found,
was blind, but now, I see.

As for Luther? Luther has a big decision to make now it's been confirmed Jesse is a match for a bone marrow transplant. I hope he makes the right one.

Every now and then I take out Marie's old letters and read them. They are a chronicle of our lives and a testament to how much Marie gave up and how much she loved us. In her letters to Charlie she always told him what we were doing and how proud she was of us.

Charlie stays in my bedroom now. He sits on a chair by the window in the daytime and I put him back in his box to sleep at night. Marie would have wanted it that way.

OTHER BOOKS BY ALICE TWIGGS VANTREASE
The Rabbit in the Moon

Alice Twiggs Vantrease lives in Savannah, Georgia where she works to support her poodles Scrabble, Pele and Hot Diggity Dog through the *designing-dogs.com* needlepoint web site. She is finally pursuing her lifelong love of writing after raising two children and retiring from running her own marketing company.